Sherlock & Irene: The Secret Truth behind 'A Scandal in Bohemia'

By Chris Chan

First edition published in 2020

Paperback ISBN 978-1-78705-614-5
ePub ISBN 978-1-78705-615-2
PDF ISBN 978-1-78705-616-9

Published by MX Publishing
335 Princess Park Manor, Royal Drive,
London, N11 3GX
www.mxpublishing.co.uk

Cover design by Brian Belanger

Contents

To: My parents, Drs. Carlyle and Patricia Chan

INTRODUCTION

The 'Great Game' Goes into Overtime

Sherlock Holmes fans have a long history of performing their own investigations into the sleuth's cases. Discrepancies in the chronology, confusing statements, and unanswered questions from the original Canon have sparked the interest of many Sherlockian scholars. Monsignor Ronald Knox, Christopher Morley, Dorothy L. Sayers, and Vincent Starrett are among the most famous and influential writers who have delved beyond the surface of the Holmes mysteries in order to clear up points in the Canon.

Many legendary mystery writers have devoted their time and talent to this exercise. Sayers famously provided a novel explanation for why Mrs. Watson once referred to her husband as "James" when faithful readers know that his first name is "John." (Sayers suggested it was an Anglicization of the good doctor's middle name, "Hamish.") Rex Stout, the creator of Nero Wolfe and Archie Goodwin, crafted the infamous essay "Watson Was a Woman," which questioned the gender of the famous narrator.

Monsignor Knox is often cited as, if not the true founder, then at least the early moving spirit of Sherlockian literary investigations and mental gymnastics. Knox used his explorations of the unsolved mysteries in the Canon to satirize the trendy New Criticism of the Bible, starting with his famous essay "Studies in the Literature of Sherlock Holmes." This was widely seen as the beginning of the popularization of "The Great Game," also known as "The Sherlockian Game," "The Holmesian Game," and more bluntly, "pseudoscholarship." Knox explored the pasts of various characters in "The Mathematics of Mrs. Watson" and suggested that the great detective's sedentary brother might have a more sinister side in "The Mystery of Mycroft."

When Sir Arthur Conan Doyle learned of Knox's efforts, he declared that, "I cannot help writing to you to tell you of the amusement – and also the amazement – with which I read your article on Sherlock Holmes. That anyone should spend such pains on such material was what surprised me."

Were Doyle were to see the vast quantities of intelligent people who have played The Great Game over the decades, he would be astounded. *The Baker*

Street Journal is full of articles covering Sherlockian scholarship and pseudoscholarship, and the BBC modernization of the Holmes universe, *Sherlock,* occasionally integrated some famous theories into their scripts, even going so far as to name the third episode of its first season "The Great Game."

With The Great Game being played for over a century with varying degrees of seriousness, one might be excused for thinking that everything that can possibly be studied about the Canon has already been addressed. This commonly-held assumption, though understandable, is flat-out wrong. There is so much in the Canon that requires additional study to make sense, and so much that does not hold up under intense scrutiny, that Sherlockian scholars are likely to have material for playing The Great Game for generations to come.

It is the intention of this monograph to apply the principles of The Great Game and Sherlockian pseudoscholarship to a point that may call into question the relationship between Sherlock Holmes and one of the most famous one-shot characters in the entire Canon: Irene Adler. Adler, also known as "*The* Woman,*" appeared in only one short story, "A

Scandal in Bohemia," and was very briefly or obliquely referenced in a handful of other tales. Nevertheless, she bears a major role in the public imagination because of a couple of unique characteristics. First, she is one of very few members of the female sex whom Holmes holds in high regard. Second, she holds the distinction of actually having outwitted Holmes, having thwarted his attempts to retrieve an incriminating photograph from her in order to protect the reputation and upcoming marriage of the King of Bohemia. As she is not really a criminal, and is arguably the wronged party in the whole scandal, Irene Adler is often seen as a sympathetic character, one who deservedly found happiness and scored a victory for herself – and her entire sex – by defending her own interests so capably.

By most assessments, "A Scandal in Bohemia" is not Sherlock Holmes' finest hour, due to his initially taking the side of a powerful man who proves to be a snob and a cad, and also because of his ultimate failure to achieve his objectives. But did Holmes fail? Upon a careful reading of "A Scandal in Bohemia," it soon becomes clear that there is much more to the story than initially meets the eye. Instead of Holmes being defeated by his own overconfidence, a more critical approach to reading the story, and reading between the lines, indicates that his ultimate goal was not to steal the photograph in question, that Holmes was playing his own game all the time, and that the entire affair turned out exactly according to plan. It further becomes evident that Holmes had a vested interest in making everybody else believe that Adler had outsmarted him, so the sleuth not only fooled the King of Bohemia, but he also pulled the wool over the eyes of his dearest friend and Boswell, Doctor Watson. Holmes essentially threw the case of "A Scandal in Bohemia."

In this monograph, I will delve into "A Scandal in Bohemia" and explore unprecedented depths, identifying statements that do not hold up under close scrutiny, and explaining why the conventional version of events is sorely lacking. I will then explain how my revised view of the narrative not only resolves these shortcomings but also shows how the events of "A Scandal in Bohemia" are tied into Holmes' role in preserving the safety and stability of not just the Bohemian monarchy, but all of Europe as well.

In the end, I seek to prove that while Sherlock Holmes had a high regard for the intelligence, cunning, and sangfroid of Irene Adler, his ultimate apotheosis of her comes not from the fact that she proved to be his superior in a battle of wits, but because she became the symbol of Holmes' realization that at times he had to obscure the real truth, shatter his own ego, and smear his own reputation all in the name of the greater good. "A Scandal in Bohemia" is not a story where Holmes was humbled by "*the* woman," but where he deliberately abased himself for the sake of things that were far greater than his own public image.

The "Scandal in Bohemia" Case

As a story, "A Scandal in Bohemia" is a mission rather than a mystery. There is no murder or jewel robbery to be solved, but rather, a scorned woman is threatening the upcoming marriage of a central European monarch. Holmes and Watson are carrying out a plan rather than untangling a web of intrigue, though Holmes' plan seemingly does not work out in the way that he has hoped.

At the tale's opening, Watson exposits with the information that Irene Adler holds an incomparably high place in Holmes' esteem, and that he honors her by referring to her as "*the* woman." Watson takes pains to explain that Holmes' feelings towards Adler are not of a passionate nature, and that Holmes is incapable of nurturing emotions akin to romantic love, being a creature driven by cold rationality.

It is March 20th, 1888. Watson is recently married. Holmes and Watson have drifted apart, as Watson is understandably spending most of his time with his wife, and when Holmes is not indulging in cocaine-fueled binges, he is investigating cases on his own. After visiting a patient, Watson makes an impromptu visit to Baker Street. Holmes observes his friend and makes a few quick deductions regarding the state of his married life.

Holmes shows Watson a note, which orders rather than asks Holmes to prepare for a potentially masked visitor that evening. The letter cites the fact that Holmes had recently had some success solving cases for some European royals, and suggests that he will be called upon to perform another delicate task. After examining the language in the note and the nature of the stationary, the pair conclude that the author is from the German-speaking nation of Bohemia.

An enormous, richly dressed, and masked man enters 221B. Their guest identifies himself as the Count Von Kramm, and states that what he is about to reveal must remain secret for a full two years, after which it will be acceptable for these secrets to be released to the world. Holmes and Watson agree to this stipulation, and after their guest explains that their mission is connected to the Bohemian monarchy, Holmes urges the "Count" to drop the pretense, making it clear that he knows their client is in fact the King of Bohemia. Faced with this blunt comment, the King is shaken, but unmasks himself and admits his true identity.

The King explains that the mission he is recruiting Holmes for revolves around "the well-known adventuress, Irene Adler." Adler, now about thirty years old, is a New Jersey-born opera singer. The King and Adler were once romantically involved, and the King wrote some potentially embarrassing letters to her. Adler also possesses a photograph of the pair of them. Adler refuses to turn over these documents to him, and the King's attempts to have the materials in question stolen have all failed. Adler intends to use the photograph to break up the engagement between the King and a Scandinavian princess, threatening to send the compromising image as soon as the upcoming union is publicly announced. The news release of the engagement is scheduled for three days later, and any hint of previous indiscretions will kill the planned marriage.

Holmes accepts the assignment, and the King provides him with a substantial amount of cash for funds. The next afternoon, Watson returns to Baker Street to find Holmes in the guise of an inebriated stable worker. Holmes has been conducting reconnaissance on Adler, and discovers that she lives by a set routine, and has a gentleman friend in the lawyer Godfrey Norton. Holmes follows Adler and Norton to a church, where he is unexpectedly and forcibly called to be a witness to the marriage of Adler and Norton.

After overhearing that Adler intends to stick to her usual routine that evening, Holmes uses the next couple of hours to set up a plan. Watson agrees to help, and Holmes gives his friend a plumber's smoke rocket, which he asks Watson to throw into Adler's house, shout out "fire," and then leave. Holmes then disguises himself as an amiable Nonconformist clergyman, and soon the pair head to Adler's house, where a small band of people recruited by Holmes has gathered.

Once Adler arrives, Holmes' allies pretend to attack her, but the disguised Holmes rushes to her rescue, and collapses after pretending to be struck by the mob. Other people working for Holmes rush forward to disperse the assailants, and Adler allows them to bring the "injured" Holmes into her home. After some brief moral misgivings, Watson carries out the plan, and Adler's sitting-room fills with smoke. Watson hurries away as the people on the street make a fuss, and ten minutes later Holmes rejoins him.

As they walk back to Baker Street, Holmes confirms that everyone on the street was hired by him, and that the purpose of the smoke-rocket was to make Adler believe her house was on fire, leading her to retrieve her most prized possession: the photograph. Adler almost withdrew the picture from behind a sliding-panel in one wall, but Holmes declared that there was no real fire. Adler, upon seeing the smoke-rocket, left the room and was not seen again. Holmes did not take the photograph at that moment, as a coachman was watching him, and instead professed himself to be recovered and left the house.

Holmes announces his plans to take the King to Adler's house early the next morning to retrieve the photograph. As the pair re-enter 221B, an unknown person wishes Holmes "good-night," and though Holmes recognizes the voice, he cannot place it.

When Holmes, Watson, and the King arrive at Adler's house the following day, the housekeeper informs them that Adler and her new husband have left for the Continent early that morning, and do not intend to come back to England. When the trio looks behind the sliding-panel, they find a letter from Adler, explaining how she came to suspect trickery, and quickly disguised herself as a young man and followed Holmes and Watson, overhearing their conversation. Knowing his plan, she decided to take the incriminating photograph and flee with her husband. Adler states that she has no further desire to get revenge on the king, and will hold onto the photograph simply as insurance to prevent the King from seeking retribution. In addition to this letter, Adler leaves behind a photograph of herself.

The King is impressed by her actions, while Holmes has become rather hostile to the King. The King declares the matter closed, trusting that his secret is safe. Instead of accepting the payment of an emerald snake ring proffered by the King, Holmes asks for the photograph as a memento, and leaves the room without shaking the King's hand.

In the concluding paragraph, Watson comments on how Holmes has not spoken disparagingly of female intellect since the Adler case, and that when Holmes mentions Adler, he invariably calls her "*the* woman."

This is the story of Holmes' most notable failure, and the only one where a clever antagonist – a woman, no less – completely defeats him. It's a story where the hero is humbled and forced to evaluate the morality of his own actions. But could there be more to this story? There are so many contradictions and unanswered questions, that it soon becomes clear that this narrative must not be taken at face value, and that "A Scandal in Bohemia" may not be a failure for Holmes after all.

Why Would 'A Scandal in Bohemia' Be the First Holmes Short Story Published?

Let us consider Doctor Watson's publication history. He wrote a full-length book recounting how he first met Sherlock Holmes and their first investigation together in *A Study in Scarlet*. His next published work was another full-length book, *The Sign of Four*. There were other cases the pair solved together during that time; perhaps Watson believed that a longer narrative would reach a wider audience, which is why he devoted his time to recounting one of the few cases that could justifiably fill an entire book on its own.

Eventually, due to the fact that most of his cases with Holmes could be told in a much shorter narrative, Watson would begin to write briefer accounts for *The Strand*, published through his literary agent Arthur Conan Doyle, before they were later compiled into *The Adventures of Sherlock Holmes* and other anthologies. Anybody who reads Watson's work knows that he has a flair for crafting a story, filling it with intrigue and suspense, and entertaining an audience. Surely, as he was publishing his stories and assembling them into a collection, he would have put some thought into which order he was listing the cases, and how this arrangement might affect his readers.

After a bit of reflection, it seems like an unusual decision for "A Scandal in Bohemia" to be the first story in an anthology. Readers may not have been familiar with *A Study in Scarlet* or *The Sign of Four*, so these short tales were possibly the first introduction many people had to Holmes. As the dates in *The Adventures of Sherlock Holmes* and later anthologies illustrate, Watson felt no need to publish Holmes' cases in chronological order. Therefore, he had the option of arranging the accounts in the collection in any order he desired, though a few tales contained brief callbacks to earlier investigations that would either require chronological ordering to avoid confusion, or these references could be easily deleted for clarity.

Almost any case could have been placed first in *The Adventures of Sherlock Holmes*. Why start with an account of Holmes' most notable failure, and one where the rightness of his cause is suspect? It puts the hero of the stories in a poor light, one which some readers might never be able to overcome when reading future tales. Why not make, say, *The Speckled Band* the first story in the collection? Chronologically, it occurred well before "A Scandal in Bohemia." It's suspenseful, atmospheric, memorable, features an impressive villain and a purely sympathetic damsel in distress, and what's more, Holmes and Watson come across as full-fledged heroes who are fully willing to risk their lives to protect a client. A savvy writer would know that in order to grab readers' attentions and loyalties, it's best to start by painting your hero in the best possible light, and saving revelations of failures and flaws until sometime later, when the fickle public is far more willing to forgive a would-be superhuman figure for being fallible on occasion. Bluntly stated, "A Scandal in Bohemia" is an odd choice to start an anthology, unless one had special reasons for giving it such a distinction.

Watson, being an extremely honest man, may have felt it his duty, simply for the purposes of posterity and accuracy, to list one of Holmes's exceedingly rare failures in his collection. But why would a case where Holmes comes off as second-best receive pride of place in the anthology? When Captain Arthur Hastings, the longtime chronicler of Hercule Poirot's investigations, compiled his first anthology of short accounts of Poirot's cases in *Poirot Investigates*, his tale "The Chocolate Box," an account of Poirot's one and only total failure, where he accused the wrong person of murder, was not anthologized in book form until the 1970s in his native England (though it did appear in a periodical before that). When "The Chocolate Box" was published in America in the 1920s, it was in a different edition of *Poirot Investigates* that featured three stories including "The Chocolate Box" that did not appear in the English edition. The American publishers printed the story of Poirot's great mistake at the very end of the collection.

It is a matter of showmanship – make the protagonist appear as impressive as possible, and save the shortcomings and failures until later, when the hero's reputation is already accepted by the reading public. "A Scandal in Bohemia" should have been saved for later in *The Adventures of Sherlock Holmes*. So why was it given pride of place, painting Holmes in one of the weakest lights he is ever shown in throughout the Canon? It seems as if when Watson compiled the collection, he made a point of making sure that the story would catch the most attention possible. But Watson, though he was an honest chronicler, would never allow his best friend to be embarrassed publicly. Unless... Holmes asked him to do so. Why would the great detective do that? It seems like he wanted people to know what happened in "A Scandal in Bohemia." But what agenda could Holmes have had in doing that?

Was the Photograph Really That Damaging?

Early in "A Scandal in Bohemia," Holmes and the King have the following exchange over the materials in Adler's possession:

"Your Majesty, as I understand, became entangled with this young person, wrote her some compromising letters, and is now desirous of getting those letters back."

"Precisely so. But how —"

"Was there a secret marriage?"

"None."

"No legal papers or certificates?"

"None."

"Then I fail to follow your Majesty. If this young person should produce her letters for blackmailing or other purposes, how is she to prove their authenticity?"

"There is the writing."

"Pooh, pooh! Forgery."

"My private note-paper."

"Stolen."

"My own seal."

"Imitated."

"My photograph."

"Bought."

"We were both in the photograph."

"Oh, dear! That is very bad! Your Majesty has indeed committed an indiscretion."

In his initial meeting with the King, Holmes notes that he is aware of the King's incriminating letters to Adler, though Holmes creates an unanswered mystery of his own by displaying his knowledge of the correspondence and failing to make it clear how he came across this top-secret bit of information. The King notes that Holmes is probably aware of Adler's existence as she is a minor celebrity, but is amazed that he knows about the letters. Notably, Holmes makes no mention of the photograph, and does not appear to have any knowledge of it until the King mentions it after Holmes explains how all of the King's personal written letters may be explained away as ersatz. It's notable that Holmes does not apply similar ideas to potentially discrediting the photograph. From the ensuing dialogue, it seems as if Adler realizes that a picture is worth a thousand words, because assuming that the King has chosen his words correctly in his conversation with Holmes, she only intends to send the photograph to the Scandinavian royals, and apparently is keeping the letters to herself.

Holmes later asks the King if the photograph were a "cabinet." A cabinet was a certain kind of sepia or black-and-white photograph, affixed to sturdier cardboard, and usually a little over six inches by a bit more than four inches in size. This made them larger and clearer than most photographs. Often a bit of information about the developer was printed on the cardboard next to the picture. The initial photograph was taken on a glass photographic plate, which resides somewhere, most likely in the records of the person who developed the picture. It's surprising that the King has not mentioned either the continued existence of the glass negative or the fact that he's already tracked down the negative and smashed it into a thousand pieces. After all, if it exists, all Irene Adler has to do is send a letter to the developer and ask him to prepare another dozen copies of the picture for her.

Actually, why hasn't she done so already? According to the King, all of Adler's leverage lies in the existence of a single photograph. Before she made her announcement, wouldn't it have made sense for her to have made as many copies of the photograph as possible, and hidden them in various locations for safekeeping, possibly leaving some in the care of lawyers to be sent to the Scandinavian royal family or published in the newspapers if anything happened to her? A woman as intelligent as Adler would know to back up her evidence. It doesn't make sense. Even if the original negative were shattered, she could have copies made, or even photograph the photograph. There was no reason to assume that stealing the one definitely known photograph would nip the scandal in the bud. Stealing it would more likely than not have done no good and more likely would've done harm by provoking Adler to make the picture public. Surely Holmes would've realized that. But if he did, then he'd know that all of his efforts were futile... unless they were all part of an elaborate charade. This train of thought will be addressed soon in another chapter.

If the theft of the photograph was not going to help, discrediting the photograph would be much more effective. As a matter of fact, while a picture is metaphorically worth a thousand words, there is no reason why a photograph, even one taken during the late nineteenth century, ought to be considered more conclusive evidence than any of the other documents. As Holmes says, handwriting can be forged, note-paper stolen, and a seal can be easily duplicated by using clay or plaster to make a mold of an indentation in wax, thereby creating a duplicate seal. But as for photographs, what is to say that the man in the photograph is not truly the King, but simply a lookalike? In the days before sophisticated technology could examine every muscle in a face and determine whether two images were of the same person or not, all it would take is to find someone of similar size and features to the King. A bit of makeup or putty and a wig might take care of any remaining dissimilarities. Simply pay the made-up duplicate a big wad of cash to tell the world that Adler hired him to pose in that picture, and voilà – the photograph is discredited, just like the letters would be with accusations of forged handwriting, duplicated seals, and stolen note-paper.

Furthermore, long before Photoshop and other means of digital image manipulation, there were many examples of false images being created through altering and combining photographs, such as a famous 1893 multiple-exposure image of a man photographing himself, created by combining images. A skilled practitioner of the photographic arts could conceivably create a comparable image of any two people, given sufficient photographs as source material. By hiring a photographic manipulator to create similar faked images, the King could potentially discredit Adler's photograph. Bottom line, all it would take is one massive bluff to cast reasonable doubt on all of Adler's claims.

Of course, all of this begs the question, what exactly was in this photograph anyway? Given the nature of cabinet photographs, which required the subjects to be still to assure a clear photo, it's unlikely that the King was unaware that the photo was taken. We can almost certainly rule out the idea that while the King and Adler were physically enjoying the pleasures of each other's company, a confederate of

Adler's was in the next room, taking a picture of them *in flagrante delicto* through a hole in the wall. With the photographic technology of the time, this wouldn't produce a clear image, and it's unlikely that they could've posed long enough to assure the capture of both of their faces. Perhaps an image of the pair hugging or Adler sitting in the King's lap was all that we can reasonably expect to have appeared in the photograph. Irene Adler simply didn't have access to the kind of photographic materials that lead to the problem of "revenge porn" in breakups today. The worst that could be in the photograph is that the two of them might be posed together, possibly hugging or kissing. It might be inferred that the relationship between the two figures in the picture was romantic, but really, did the Scandinavian royal family genuinely expect a monarch to reach the age of thirty without so much as a girlfriend? Since the photograph probably couldn't contain anything really shocking, and could be easily discredited, how dangerous could it be?

The more one thinks about it, the less problematic a photograph purporting to be of Adler and the King might be. There is one other possibility that raises some concerns. What if there were something else in the photograph, some notable image besides Adler and the King that could be inflammatory? It's something to consider. But if so, then that means that the King is being less than honest with Holmes about the nature of the photograph, and quite possibly about Adler's motives as well.

Why Would the King Trust Burglars?

The many contradictions and unanswered questions in the King's statements to Holmes illustrate that the King is hiding something, which calls his motives into question. One of these problems lies in the need for secrecy. Throughout his first conversation with Holmes, the King explains that this whole matter must be kept absolutely quiet, and then subtly contradicts himself moments later.

In his initial meeting with Holmes, the King explains the reasons why he came to London under the flimsy guise of a mask and sobriquet. The King explains that he couldn't delegate hiring Holmes to a subordinate, declaring that, "you can understand that I am not accustomed to doing such business in my own person. Yet the matter was so delicate that I could not confide it to an agent without putting myself in his power." All well and good. This makes perfect sense – the King had no servant or friend who could be trusted with such a sensitive situation, as everyone in his circle was likely to either blackmail or otherwise manipulate the King after learning about the liaison.

Of course, after a little thought, it is obvious that there are already people who might know about the King's secret. For example, the King and Adler lived before the time of selfies. Someone had to take the picture of the two of them. That photographer and possibly the developer, if the two are not the same person, knew about the relationship, and could potentially be hazards to the King, unless they have passed away since the photo was taken. Why are these potential leaks not mentioned? Possibly the King has already taken drastic steps to silence these people, and Holmes, realizing this, discretely stays silent, but is on his guard against the King, knowing that he and Watson are potentially loose ends for the monarch.

Not only that, but by the King's own admission, he has put other, potentially untrustworthy people in positions where they could soon gain mastery over him. When talking about his previous attempts to retrieve the papers, he states that, "Five attempts have been made. Twice burglars in my pay ransacked her house. Once we diverted her luggage when she travelled. Twice she has been waylaid. There has been no result." That means that burglars or other paid thugs have been recruited to steal the documents in question. But this contradicts the King's earlier statement about the need for extreme secrecy. If he could not trust anyone in his acquaintance to come to Holmes, how could he place his fate in the hands of hired goons?

The burglars in his employment were probably trained criminals, which would be an immediate red flag for their trustworthiness. Yet in order for them to do their job, the King would have to tell them what they were looking for, and describe it thoroughly. The King couldn't just refer to "a photograph," as the burglars might triumphantly return bearing a snapshot of Adler's maiden aunt and her cats. The King would need to explain that the image would be of himself and Adler, and probably describe the content of the letters as well, or at least identify his notepaper and admit that the missives contained sensitive material. In essence, the King would be turning his deepest secret over to potential extortionists.

It is certainly not too much of a stretch to postulate that if the burglars actually did find the picture, they would immediately blackmail the King for enormous sums, or perhaps even sell the papers to the highest bidder. Even if the King tried to bend the burglars to his will, such as by holding their family members hostage until the papers were turned over to him, the burglars would still have the edge, as they would remind the King that the fate of Europe lies upon his shoulders, and if anything were to happen to their families, the Bohemian monarchy would never recover from the forthcoming scandal. In any event, the burglars would no doubt figure out that they would be loose ends, and that the King could not risk leaving them alive and potentially sharing the information they'd learned. The burglars would know that the moment they placed the papers in the King's hands, they would have signed their own death warrants.

In short, the King is contradicting himself regarding the level of secrecy and the papers. First he says he cannot trust his closest friends and advisors, and then he says that he has put himself in the hands of professional thieves? It does not make sense.

Let us then consider the King's statements critically. The description of the five attempts to retrieve the papers seems too specific to be made up of whole cloth. Let us then accept that five attempts *have* been made to retrieve the papers. Therefore, the King trusted the agents sent to retrieve the materials. Therefore, if they can be trusted with this information, they could have been trusted to come to Holmes. Therefore, on the face of it, there was no reason for the King to take the security risk and come to Holmes himself.

The king's story contradicts itself. It therefore seems as if there's a darker truth behind his initial story. A theory about the King's true motives will be discussed later on in this study.

Why Didn't Holmes Take the Picture and Run?

Upon reading "A Scandal in Bohemia" carefully, it becomes clear that it would have been really easy for Holmes to have succeeded in his objective of retrieving the photograph. He knew where it was hidden. He was just a few yards away from it. Why didn't he grab the picture and go? When describing what happened after Watson threw the smoke-rocket, he says,

> *"The alarm of fire was admirably done. The smoke and shouting were enough to shake nerves of steel. She responded beautifully. The photograph is in a recess behind a sliding panel just above the right bell-pull. She was there in an instant, and I caught a glimpse of it as she half-drew it out. When I cried out that it was a false alarm, she replaced it, glanced at the rocket, rushed from the room, and I have not seen her since. I rose, and, making my excuses, escaped from the house. I hesitated whether to*

attempt to secure the photograph at once; but the coachman had come in, and as he was watching me narrowly it seemed safer to wait. A little over-precipitance may ruin all."

A little over-precipitance might ruin all in some circumstances, but a bit of dawdling may bring disaster. Holmes delayed for about twelve hours, and that allowed Adler to grab the photograph and get out of Dodge. This was a fatal mistake. Why did Holmes make it? In the standard reading of the story, Holmes was complacent and severely underestimated his opponent. He never dreamt that Adler would smell a rat, and he certainly never suspected that she would find a way to figure out what his plans were. Thus, Holmes' misogyny and arrogance proved to be his downfall.

The only problem with this interpretation of the story is that for it to have happened as described, Holmes has to be worse than sexist. He has to be a complete fool as well. After all, Holmes knows that Adler considers the photograph to be her most prized possession, and her revenge and perhaps even her life depend on her keeping it intact and safe. Consider, if you will, the series of events that Irene Adler experienced in the space of less than three minutes. First, she's caught up in a street-fight and nearly injured as soon as she leaves her carriage. Second, a clergyman she's never met before tries to save her. Third, the clergyman is seriously injured, and the wounded man is carried into her house and left in her sitting-room. Fourth, her home suddenly fills with smoke and people in the street call out "fire." This takes place a moment after her maid opened the window after the presumably injured man gesticulated for fresh air. Now, I'll cheerfully concede that that London is known for its thick fog, and coal-smoke was a major environmental problem in London for many decades, but surely a lot of smoke filling up one's sitting-room at a moment's notice was not an everyday occurrence (assuming, of course, that one kept one's chimneys regularly swept). Holmes was unlikely to have been able to lunge for the smoke-rocket and hide it before Adler saw it – not without breaking his cover as an injured, elderly man. Adler was likely to have seen the smoke-rocket, realized that this was no random event or practical joke, and smelt a rat. Fifth, the fact that a man supposedly on the edge of death could regain consciousness and clarity enough to declare a "false alarm" is a dead giveaway that the man isn't as badly harmed as it seems at first.

Put all of these together, and Holmes' plan is easily exposed as the ruse it was. Up until the smoke-rocket, even the least gullible mind might accept the early events of the evening as a random act of violence. Indeed, Adler states in her final letter to Holmes that, "Until after the alarm of fire, I had not a suspicion." Holmes has a fairly good understanding of how people respond and why. He knew that given the circumstances, with Adler's adrenaline pumping after nearly becoming a victim of violence herself, and concern for the life of a man who was injured trying to help her racing through her mind, the threat of fire would be enough to make even the toughest, most jaded, and perceptive mind panic and act on impulse – as indeed, Adler did. The ruse was a cleverly crafted drama designed to promote emotional manipulation leading to thoughtless behavior... up to a point.

Magicians and dramatists know that there's a psychological moment when it comes to shaping people's minds and actions. People can be influenced by stimuli for a certain period of time, but after a certain point the spell is broken and critical thinking skills start to pierce the veil of deception. If the audience *wants* to believe in the web being woven, such as an audience who has paid money expecting to be amazed, befuddled, or entertained, then it's easier to keep the atmosphere going. But when a person is already on his or her guard for being manipulated, like Irene Adler, who knew for a fact that her nemesis the King was almost certainly going to pull something very soon to get his grubby royal hands on the letters and photograph, all it takes is a slight incongruity to yank someone out of their mesmerized state. Immediately, suspicion enters their minds again, especially in the case of an intelligent person who has had reason to distrust people in the past.

Up to the moment where Adler revealed the hiding-place of the photograph, Holmes' plan was actually pretty clever. The problem is that it while was an excellent scheme to *reveal* the location of Adler's cache of sensitive material, it was not an effective long con to fool a target. Like many high-paced action movies, it's easy to get caught up in two hours of shootings, car chases, and explosions; and be entertained in a violent and suspenseful world. The only problem is the slightest break in the action will give the audience members a chance to turn their brains back on and start thinking once again. And once the little gray cells start functioning again, it's pretty easy to pick up on all of the plot holes, contradictions, and general stupidity that fills the movie. Once the spell is broken and the viewer stops viewing the movie as a fun entertainment and starts seeing it as an idiotic mess of shoddy writing, the experience is ruined. Instead of being an amusing diversion, the movie becomes a frustrating waste of time and money. It's hard to create a well-crafted script that will keep the audience enthralled based on quality plotting, characterization, and dialogue. Screenplays like that are hard to come by, which is why most action movies realize that the only way to keep the audience from realizing what other dreck they're spending hundreds of millions of dollars to produce is to keep their viewers distracted by frequent shots of random objects blowing up, and the ever-popular close-ups of scantily clad or even totally naked attractive people. Overload with stimuli, and you can keep the spell going for a surprisingly long time. Give the audience a chance to think by stopping the action or boring them with actual dialogue, and these viewers will probably cease to enjoy the film.

It's that principle that needs to be applied here. Holmes knew that he could fool Adler for a few minutes. He should have realized that the deception wouldn't remain convincing for twelve full hours. Fortunately, he didn't need to keep Adler fooled for twelve hours, or even twelve minutes. Twelve seconds was all he needed. Holmes had to call out "false alarm" to provoke Adler to put the photograph back in the sliding-panel, because it wouldn't help if Adler took the photograph with her, and then hid it somewhere else after leaving the room. But from the moment Adler had the chance to actually think about the smoke in the room and her guest's outburst, her nostrils were no doubt twitching with the unmistakable odor of rat. This would only be exacerbated by the fact that the seemingly-at-death's-door clergyman left the house unaided just a few minutes later.

Of course, if Holmes was determined to keep his cover, why didn't he arrange for a pair of his allies to retrieve him after a few minutes? Dressed as ambulance attendees and bearing him away on a stretcher, Holmes could've been removed without raising eyebrows. Instead, Holmes chose a course of action that was bound to reveal that the seemingly benign clergyman wasn't all he initially appeared to be.

All of this would be no serious problem if Holmes seized his first opportunity to grab the photograph. The photograph was in the same room as he was, and the only other person in the room was John, the coachman. What was to stop Holmes from leaping up, sprinting across the room, and snatching the papers from the hiding-place? Nothing at all, really. The coachman might've been too stunned to respond at first. And then what? It's unclear how many exits there were to Adler's home, but Holmes could've easily used his knowledge of the martial art of baritsu to subdue or avoid the coachman without causing an innocent man any physical harm, and then rushed out the door. Or he could have leapt out the open window. If worst came to worst and all escape routes were somehow barred, he could've ripped the photograph to shreds. If he were absolutely determined to maintain his cover as long as possible, he could have easily distracted John the coachman using a ruse such as this one:

HOLMES. *(Groans.)* Oh sir, my heart! I'm having such terrible palpitations! *(Pats pockets.)* My pills! My doctor gave me a little bottle of pills when this happens. Please sir, they must've fallen out when I was attacked. Could you please go outside and look for them?

JOHN. I don't know. Miss Adler told me to stay here and watch you.

HOLMES. *(Gasps.)* Oh sir, you'll be watching me die! My head's swimming, and I think my heart's going to pop out of chest, it is! *(Chokes.)* I think this is it. I'm dying. If only I had my pills....

JOHN. Wait! Hold on, I'll go out and look for your pills!

Nothing could be simpler. As it stands, Holmes was in the position of the hare in Aesop's fable "The Tortoise and the Hare." All the hare had to do was keep running just a little bit longer, and he would've won the race. Instead, he napped, and the tortoise crept past him and triumphed. Not to belittle Adler, but Holmes' loss wasn't due to a woman's wit, but instead to his own procrastination. Holmes could have retrieved the photograph, but he failed due to a massive error of judgement.

Or was it? These mistakes are so glaring, so obvious, that it seems that a man of Holmes' cleverness could not possibly have made them inadvertently. There is a very strong case to be made that they were deliberate. Suppose that Holmes purposefully sabotaged himself. He staged the whole charade in order to alert Adler and provoke her into fleeing with the photograph. Holmes wanted Adler to run off with the compromising materials all along. If we accept this supposition as true, then all of Holmes' actions suddenly make much more sense. They were not foolish mistakes, but instead were part of a very cunning plan. But what could have been the purpose of such a plan? More confounding aspects of "A Scandal in Bohemia" have to be explored before moving forward with this question.

Why Did Holmes Discuss Sensitive Information With Watson on the Street?

Holmes knew that he was dealing with sensitive matters of international importance, yet he chose to talk about them while walking on the street with Watson, where any passersby could overhear him, as indeed, one did. Why, when some big-eared ne'er-do-well could easily pick up some critical information and twist it to his own purposes, did Holmes not tell Watson to just wait five minutes, and they would discuss everything in the comfort and security of 221B Baker Street?

The WWII security slogan "loose lips sink ships" is applicable here. Holmes' ploy to get Adler to reveal her hiding place worked, although as a direct consequence of his dramatic strategy, Adler's suspicions were triggered. Still, while she now believed it was likely that an agent of the King was now after her papers, she didn't know for certain who was behind the attempt, nor did she even know if he'd done anything to the photograph or not. Fortunately for Adler, Holmes provided her with all of the information she needed. The picture was still at her home, he described his entire strategy, and stated when he was returning with the King to seize the photograph. Holmes' conversation with Watson was full of specific details of his plans, and served as a detailed warning for Adler.

It is unclear from Watson's account whether or not it was exceptionally easy for the disguised Adler to follow him. Watson notes that ten minutes after throwing the rocket, his friend rejoined him, and they walked in silence for a few minutes before Holmes started explaining everything. It is not made certain whether or not Holmes was still wearing his clergyman's costume. It might have been wise for Holmes to duck into an alley at an early opportunity, and swiftly remove his distinctive coat and hat, which made it far easier for anyone to trail him, and replace them with different outerwear. After all, nothing could be simpler than to have one of his paid allies waiting for him with the change of clothes. To swap coats and hats would take less than half a minute, and Holmes could meet up with his friend, easy in the knowledge that he'd taken steps to shake off any potential pursuers.

But we don't know if Holmes took that elementary precaution. Perhaps he remained in his

Nonconformist clergyman costume. Wearing distinctive attire would certainly make it easier for anyone to follow him. In Sidney Paget's original illustration of Holmes and Watson's return to Baker Street, Holmes is still wearing the clergyman outfit, though again, there's no conclusive evidence for this in the text. The vital point is this. If Holmes were still disguised, then someone addressing him as "Mr. Sherlock Holmes" ought to have set off red flags. How could someone have recognized him in disguise, unless they'd already seen through his charade or overheard him? If Holmes were still wearing his costume, Holmes ought to have known that someone calling out to him by name was a danger signal... unless he knew that he had no reason to fear.

There is a clear and simple answer to why Holmes allowed himself to commit such a grievous breach of security, and why he didn't panic when his cover was blown, and when this explanation is accepted, it completely turns our understanding of Holmes' motives and goals in the Bohemia case upside-down. Holmes was aware that Adler was behind them, and he wanted her to overhear everything. He knew she suspected him, and once he'd assured himself that she was behind them (perhaps he could smell her perfume, or she failed to disguise the pacing of her footsteps), and he was convinced that no other potential enemies could overhear them, he began talking to Watson, making it clear that he had not taken the photograph, summarized his plan, and explained that he would bring the King around to take the photograph the following day at eight in the morning. He told Adler everything she needed to know in order to make her plans to escape. When Adler wished him "good night," Holmes must've suppressed a smile so as not to reveal his hidden delight to Watson. He knew exactly "who the deuce that could have been." And "the woman" in question now had all the information and time she needed to flee with the incriminating documents.

We know that Holmes was not an incompetent fool. His seeming blundering was a clever feint to get Adler to run away with the photograph. This means that Holmes did not want to help the King after all. Holmes had his own agenda in this case.

Why Was Irene Adler's Drawing Room Ransacked?

When Holmes, Watson, and the King arrive at Irene Adler's home at the end of the story, "The furniture was scattered about in every direction, with dismantled shelves and open drawers, as if the lady had hurriedly ransacked them before her flight." But why would Adler's home be in such disarray?

Let's assume that Adler and her new husband were in a mad rush to leave, due to a desire to escape the King and Holmes. She had at most eight or nine hours to pack, assuming she didn't sleep. But she couldn't carry all of her possessions with her. If she were in a rush to leave, it would take no more than an hour to place the photograph and papers, her jewelry, some clothing, and a few other treasured items in a suitcase or two, especially considering that she had a housekeeper to help her. Once she had gathered all she needed and wanted, all she had to do was tell her housekeeper to pack up her remaining possessions, and have them shipped to her when she called for them. Given the time available, what needed to be packed, and the relative safety of the rest of her belongings, there is no cause for Adler to tear her drawing-room apart. Indeed, if she could not be bothered to close drawers after removing items from cabinets, why was the sliding shutter by the bell-pull closed securely? Even if she put her own photograph in the recess, if she displayed the same level of hurriedness, the shutter would likely be ajar.

The idea that Adler was in such a hurry to leave that she tore a room in her house apart simply will not hold water when one considers that at midnight, she took the time to sit down and write a letter to Holmes explaining how she uncovered his scheme. It would take at least ten minutes to write this letter, perhaps longer when one factors in dipping a pen into an inkwell, and blotting the wet ink. How could someone be in such a hurry to pack that she tears her drawing-room apart, yet she leisurely writes a missive of substantial length? If the letter were smeared and flecked with ink-spots, one might think that Watson would've mentioned that detail. And the letter does not read like the writing of a woman in a frantic hurry. Adler's letter is three hundred and thirteen words long. Had she wanted to, she could've said all she needed to in less than a hundred. Why would Adler tear around her sitting-room like a tornado, practically destroying the furniture in shelves in the process of grabbing items? Surely a woman who was sufficiently self-possessed to trail Sherlock Holmes at the spur of the moment would have the memory power to remember where she kept her possessions, so she wouldn't have to tear the room apart to get what she needed.

Logically, Adler would wait until all the possessions she intended to take with her were safely packed away, and then write the letter. That means that she managed to take care of all of her packing between the time she returned to her home after meeting with her new husband (perhaps around nine at the latest) and midnight, the time she dates the start of writing her letter to Holmes. That means she had about three hours to pack. That is more than enough time to take everything she needed in a neat and orderly manner. There is simply no good reason for Adler's drawing-room to be in such disarray.

It seems as if Watson made a false deduction. Someone ransacked Adler's house, but it wasn't the lady.

If Adler didn't tear her own home to shreds, then who did? The damage to the house indicates that the people searching the house were looking for something. (It's surprising that the noise of the rummaging around didn't wake up the housekeeper, though she may have slept in an isolated attic room or even lived off the premises.) Really, the only items in the entire building that burglars would have a vested interest in finding are the photograph and letters. And the primary person with an interest in getting those items is the King of Bohemia.

The King probably wouldn't perform this search himself – he has hired minions to perform this sort of task for him. By his own admission, he has made five attempts to retrieve the papers. Two of these times, burglars in the employment of the King tore Adler's house apart. Why not a third? If the burglars were insufficiently competent to find the papers in the past, it is totally believable that they would fail again to find the hidden panel. But why would the King order another search when Holmes promised him the papers in the morning? Why couldn't he wait? If Adler had been seen leaving the house in the middle of the night with luggage, whoever was watching her would assume she took the picture with her. Of course, Adler could have slipped out the back door in disguise with only a single satchel to carry her necessities. That would explain why the King's henchmen did not know she wasn't there.

So why would the King be in such a hurry to retrieve the papers? Possibly he didn't trust Holmes, but perhaps the King was under additional pressure to retrieve the papers. But who could have put that much pressure on a king? We only know of one person in the Canon with that power. A criminal mastermind and the head of a syndicate with the power to exert control over a monarch: Professor Moriarty. The King was actually a pawn of the Napoleon of Crime. This postulation will be expounded upon later.

Why Was the King So Relieved?

If the King's swiftly changing mood and attitude are anything to go by, then his love life may very likely be pretty volatile, which may have played a part in his breakup with Adler. For much of the narrative, the King is anxious due to the Adler situation. He professes to fear for the future of Europe, the reputation of the ruling family of Bohemia, and stresses the seriousness of the situation, quietly chastising Holmes for treating the situation dispassionately as an intellectual exercise. The King offers Holmes an initial thousand pounds for expenses, plus carte blanche for whatever else he needs, declaring that "I tell you that I would give one of the provinces of my kingdom to have that photograph."

From the King's description, the stakes couldn't possibly be any higher. The King insists on the importance of the matter and confesses to be wracked by anxiety. In contrast, Holmes is utterly confident in his ability to resolve the situation satisfactorily, and even informs the King he'll take care of a couple of other pressing cases before turning his attention to the King's problem. Interestingly and surprisingly, the King does not insist that his case come first, stressing that whatever else Holmes might want to investigate, the Bohemian matter is more important. He's content to wait his place in Holmes' queue, which seems unusual for a monarch.

A couple of days later, the King is frantic, running into 221B, grabbing Holmes by the shoulders, and showing no regal restraint as to his anxiety over the matter. When they arrive at Adler's home and find her gone, the King is despondent, declaring "all is lost." Then once they read Adler's letter, the King is completely relieved, remarking on Adler's brilliance, and professing to be one hundred percent convinced that they have nothing to fear from her. Of course, Adler says that she'll never reveal the incriminating photograph unless forced to if the King comes after her, but really, when the King gushes that "I know that her word is inviolate. The photograph is now as safe as if it were in the fire," one can't help but think he's being a trifle overoptimistic. Even if the King trusts her completely, he can't be sure that she'll always have control over the photograph, as the following chapter will discuss. His sudden acceptance of the situation, where Adler will hold this leverage over him for the rest of his life (or at least the next two years), seems like a sudden jolt. Not only that, but a King is the sort of man used to holding all the power. It seems uncharacteristic that this monarch would abruptly pivot to being happy with a situation where a spurned lover still held a trump card over him. There is no hint of the King being upset with Holmes for not fulfilling the terms of his mission.

Essentially, the King's expression of relief seems to be disproportionate to the situation, and a good deal more trepidation and anxiety would be in order. It almost seems as if the King is anxious over something other than the fate of the photograph. But what else could have happened to cause such a personality-changing sense of relief?

It should also be noted that the King has relaxed his security precautions prior to learning of Adler's escape. When he first visited Holmes at night, he wore a mask to disguise his identity, though it failed to fool Holmes. Yet in the bright daylight of morning, the King does nothing to hide his identity. Admittedly, there's no point for masking himself for

Holmes, Watson, and Adler, but what of the housekeeper or any other passersby on the streets?

Something is clearly affecting the King's emotions to cause him such unbridled relief upon reading Adler's letter, even though the situation could conceivably spiral out of Adler's control. If the King's emotional state is not due solely to assurance that the photograph is safe, perhaps the King's relief comes from the fact that he was not compelled to take certain actions that would have become necessary if there had been a difficulty with retrieving the photograph...

What If Some Other Villain Got Involved?

Upon reading Adler's final missive, the King of Bohemia is relieved, for he now believes that his former paramour will never release the photograph as long as he never tries to harm her or her husband. The situation, as far as the King is concerned, is resolved.

But is it? Even if we take this statement at face value, and believe that Adler is a woman of principle, isn't the King's relaxation a trifle premature? Suppose that before two years have passed, if her husband and perhaps her baby were deathly ill, a destitute Adler's only chance to raise the necessary funds to save her family's life would be to blackmail the King of Bohemia with the photograph, but Adler's sense of honor still prohibited her from taking such a step. That doesn't mean that someone else, someone with far fewer scruples, wouldn't leap at the opportunity to take advantage of the potential wealth and power that would result from a careful parlaying of the photograph.

After all, a lot can happen in the two years that the King said needed to pass before this matter could be talked about freely. It's possible that once the

King is safely married, and an heir is on the way, that the photograph loses its power. But there's many a slip between cup and lip, and the King still isn't married yet. Until the wedding (possibly later if an annulment is possible), the photograph is still dynamite. What if a blackmailer like Charles Augustus Milverton hired one of Adler's domestic servants to obtain the crucial papers? The fuse may not be lit, but any number of circumstances could have set off the metaphorical bomb.

Let us look at a theoretical situation. Professor Moriarty becomes aware of the photograph's existence and what it means for the King of Bohemia. Surely the Napoleon of Crime would leap at the chance to snatch up a bargaining chip that could potentially drain the Bohemian coffers, manipulate trade deals to his benefit, or even affect international relations? Carefully utilizing the photograph and manipulating the potential fallout of a scandal, Moriarty could become the de facto ruler of Bohemia, making the King his puppet. It's a power play that a criminal mastermind couldn't possibly resist. And even if Watson never recorded this adventure to paper, it's still possible that rumors of the photograph's existence could have filtered out from the Bohemian court and into Moriarty's web of crime.

With the cleverest and most able thieves at his disposal, it's quite likely that Moriarty could succeed where the King's minions failed, and track down Adler, locate the photograph, and steal it from her. Indeed, Adler now has an Achilles' heel that she did not previously possess. If someone were to kidnap her beloved husband and threaten him with harm should Adler not turn over the photograph, Adler might well have no choice but to surrender her piece of leverage. Ultimately, there are infinite ways that a clever criminal or even a brutal bungler could get hold of an image with the potential to alter the balance of power in Europe. The King of Bohemia is probably not the brightest diamond in the crown, evidenced by the fact that he either posed for the photograph that would become his downfall or at the very least put himself in a position that could undermine the future of his own reign and his nation, so we can safely accept the possibility that he lacks the foresight to realize just what a perilous situation might lie at some point down the road. Similarly,

Watson, though no fool, has such an honest mental make-up that he might fail to see the potential implications of what could happen to the photograph in the future.

But Holmes? Surely his great brain could – and almost certainly did – see that "A Scandal in Bohemia" might have a devastating sequel. Why didn't he say anything? Why didn't he do anything? These questions can be explained by noting that he wisely decided that it was best to keep this potentially devastating contingency to himself, and it's probable that he did take steps to address the situation, though secretly, in a way that Watson never knew.

Was Irene Adler Really a Blackmailer?

If the King's attitude is changeable, then if the events of the story are anything to go by, Adler's attitude is even more so. In the opening scene, the King insists that Adler's "soul of steel" drives her to go to any lengths to prevent the King from marrying another woman. According to the King, Adler is obsessed with revenge and humiliating the King, even if it leads to the destabilization of European politics. From the King's description, Adler is a bitter and obsessed ex-, out for blood and refusing to see reason, dangling the Victorian-era equivalent of revenge porn over him.

Yet as the story progresses, what we learn about Adler doesn't match the King's comments. Her behavior simply doesn't match the mindset of the sort of woman she's accused of being. Her life is "quiet" in Holmes' estimation, consisting of regular evening outings and singing at concerts. One would think that if she were devoting her life to extortion in a potentially dangerous power play, knowing that an extremely powerful man with substantial resources was after her and a document in her possession, she would find a place to hide where the King and his minions were less likely to track her down, perhaps even taking the rudimentary precaution of using a false name. Sticking to a regular schedule only makes her an easier target for capture, or leaving her home unguarded for burglars to search and plunder. As mentioned earlier, Adler really ought to have taken the rudimentary precaution of making as many copies of her photograph as possible and hiding them in secured locations, that is, if she were really plotting to release the documents.

She's also in a relationship with the lawyer, Godfrey Norton, which throws her attitude towards the King into question. Her ostensible motive in blackmailing the King is to prevent his marriage, supposedly out of revenge for his treatment of her. One might reasonably be surprised that she would be distracted by her vengeance plans to pursue a relationship, reasoning that she was so badly treated by the King that she would have been reluctant or too traumatized to begin dating again. In any event, Adler ought to have been sufficiently savvy to realize that anyone she was in a relationship with would become a target, and might have to upend his life in order to be with her, as indeed Norton was compelled to do.

It's notable that the King is utterly unaware of Adler's relationship with Norton. Despite having sent numerous agents after the photograph, none of them has ever found out about the relationship, which Holmes uncovered in less than a day with extreme ease. The King's reactions on the way to Adler's home paint him as a man who seemed completely blindsided by the possibility that his ex- might have gotten over him and moved on with her life. Perhaps the King was convinced that after being with the reigning monarch of Bohemia, Adler would forever be unable to harbor romantic feelings towards another man of lowlier station. Furthermore, with the King being faced with the knowledge that he had misjudged Adler's character in this aspect, one might think that he ought to be wondering whether he really knew Adler well enough to know that she would never share the incriminating photograph. The King clearly does not have as firm a grasp of Adler's character as he claims to have.

Another critical point is that at no point in her letter to Holmes does Adler mention her plan to prevent the King's marriage, or a desire to humiliate him publicly and ruin his reputation. On the contrary, the final paragraph of the letter indicates that Adler is in fact concerned that the King means to do her harm. From the tone of her letter, Adler presents herself as acting entirely in defense of herself, as opposed to the King's account, where she has gone on the offensive to control and potentially destroy him.

In any event, it is never made clear exactly what caused Adler's supposed change of mind. Did she simply decide that her happy relationship led her to choose to forgive and move forward with her life? Or did she decide that she no longer cared about the Scandinavian princess being wed to a cad, and concluded that the people of Bohemia would be just fine with a dishonorable monarch on the throne? The King has done nothing to show he has changed or done anything to encourage Adler to put the past behind her. Adler has purportedly been holding the photograph over the King's head for months, perhaps years. Has true love managed to purge all resentment towards the King from her heart? Surely, if bitterness remained, there was nothing to stop Adler from marrying Norton and releasing the photograph out of spite. The whole objective of the alleged blackmail scheme was to prevent the King's marriage, and the way the King described the situation, that marriage would have been blocked whether he complied with her request or defied her and caused the release of the documents.

But there is something very eyebrow-raising about Adler's final letter to Holmes. At no point does she actually admit to planning to use her compromising information to force the King to do her bidding. She does declare in the last paragraph that "The King may do what he will without hindrance from one whom he has cruelly wronged." Yet she never mentions her initial plan to prevent the King's marriage. She has known for some time that the King would send an agent to come after the documents, yet in her message, she describes herself solely in terms befitting a victim who is only acting out of self-preservation. If one reads her letter critically, it will be noted that she never speaks of using the photograph in an active manner, such as by showing it to the Scandinavians, but in a defensive way, using these materials to prevent the King from coming after her. After reading Adler's final letter objectively, it seems as if Adler had been more afraid of the King than he was of her. She was not paralyzed with fear for her life, but she does write as if she were aware that danger was always a possibility. Therefore, if she were really trying to destroy the King's wedding, she would have taken more steps to protect herself from bodily harm. From Adler's words, it seems as if she simply wanted to live her regular life in peace, knowing that the possession of the incriminating documents was the only thing that kept the King from having her murdered out of fear of what she might tell the world.

As Adler never admits to blackmail, it is fair to wonder whether or not the King's initial statement to Holmes was reliable. Is it possible that Adler was never trying to extort him, and that the blackmail scheme was simply a ruse on the King's part to compel Holmes to retrieve the photograph, as Holmes would be unlikely to swipe an innocent woman's mementos simply because their existence unsettled a libertine monarch? If this is the case, then the King must have had a dark ulterior motive, and Adler was not a blackmailer, but instead was a woman who was in a delicate and hazardous position placed on her by a potentially dangerous ex-.

Who Warned Irene Adler about Sherlock Holmes?

In Adler's letter to Holmes, she makes an interesting statement: "I had been warned against you months ago. I had been told that if the King employed an agent it would certainly be you. And your address had been given me." That is an intriguing claim to make, because it provides evidence of multiple points.

First, Adler was aware of Holmes' existence and thus knew that he was her most likely opponent. We do not, however, know for certain just how much reconnaissance she performed to learn more about Holmes, if any. It seems unlikely that a woman as intelligent as Adler would be aware of a potential threat, yet do nothing to prepare for it. The comment of Adler knowing Holmes' address is notable, for she could have disguised herself and paid Holmes a visit under some pretext in order to gauge her opponent's powers. Yet she never mentions having done this, or asking anybody else to help her prepare for Holmes' investigation. That seems like an odd lack of action of Adler's part.

Second, Adler was in some doubt as to whether the King would "employ an agent" or not. This is an ambiguous phrase. If there was any doubt as to the King's actions, it seems ridiculous to assume that the King would meekly accede to her request. Indeed, Adler must be aware of the previous attempts to obtain the papers (being too perceptive to dismiss stolen luggage as an unfortunate coincidence), so she is aware of the possibility that when the King is sufficiently desperate, he will turn to a higher class of agent. Another way to read the doubt in the possibility of the King's employing an agent is that it was conceivable that the King might try to obtain the documents himself, but Adler's familiarity with the King might lead her to conclude that he's insufficiently clever or courageous to handle the matter himself.

Third, Irene Adler had an ally who was aware that Holmes was the most likely threat to her. But who was it? It's notable that Adler neglects to mention the name of her ally. Who could it be? Her domestic staff is unlikely to have the knowledge of Holmes' influence and reputation to warn her of them. Though Adler goes out to socialize at concerts,

Holmes does not uncover evidence of any close friendships. The only other person we know to have any sort of relationship with her is Godfrey Norton. On paper, he sounds like a much more promising candidate for warning Adler about Holmes. As a lawyer, he could conceivably have learned of Holmes' relationship with law enforcement and connections to powerful people. But if Norton were her source, why did she hide his name, as if she were afraid to reveal the identity of her ally? Norton's connection to her was already well-known, she might as well have said "My husband warned me…"

Who was this anonymous friend and ally to Adler? It seems like she must have some confidante with knowledge of Holmes' skills. But who could it be? Could it be some prominent person who became a fan of Adler through her singing, possibly even a memorable of some royal house of Europe? Could it be someone whose path has crossed with Holmes in the past? In any event, it must be someone whom Adler saw the need to protect, given her coyness in naming her source. In any event, we simply don't have any evidence to turn speculation into certainty.

If we do pass into pure unrestrained theory, then there is one tantalizing possibility that must be considered. There's one other person who could've warned Adler about Sherlock Holmes: Sherlock Holmes himself!

At first, this sounds utterly ludicrous, but if we adopt the theory that I have already posited, that Holmes had an ulterior motive in taking the case for the King of Bohemia, then it suddenly becomes much more plausible. Holmes may have been involved in the affairs of the King and Adler for quite some time, as his brief comment in "His Last Bow" (discussed in an upcoming chapter) illustrates. Could Holmes have been manipulating the relationship between the King and Adler for years, and the events of "A Scandal in Bohemia" were actually the capstone of a long-term delicate project of international intrigue? As the following chapters will posit, Holmes may have had a vested interest in making Adler aware of his existence and potential influence, and surreptitiously warned Adler about himself in a way that would make her hesitant to reveal her source.

Holmes the Sore Loser?

One of the great aspects of Sherlock Holmes' character is that he is neither a sycophant nor a snob. He puts the same level of effort into investigating a case brought forward to him by an unemployed young woman facing the prospect of penury that he does in taking on a job from a titled nobleman. He has been known to tweak the noses of prominent civil servants and diplomats with dramatic practical jokes and barbed quips, and he has been known to give the misbehaving wealthy a severe tongue-lashing when the situation called for it.

Holmes frequently takes on matters of national and international importance. He is not a diplomat, but his brother Mycroft has stressed the need for tact and care in certain delicate cases connected to Britain's global interests. Holmes may not share a leader's political views or respect that monarch's behavior in private life, but he does not allow his personal dislike to interfere with the greater good. Holmes is irregular in the rewards he accepts from royalty, taking a jeweled ring from the reigning family of Holland for an undisclosed investigation and an emerald tie-pin from a "gracious lady" at

Windsor for his service in "The Bruce-Partington Plans," but declining a knighthood for a top-secret case taken around the time of "The Three Garridebs." All three of these cases are presumably successes, so Holmes therefore has no qualms about flaunting the trophies of his triumphs.

One can understand Holmes declining a rich reward for a case that he personally considered a failure, even if his prominent client were completely pleased with the result. That may explain why Holmes declined the emerald snake-ring offered to him at the end of "A Scandal in Bohemia," but it does not account for the fact that by "A Case of Identity," he has accepted an old gold snuffbox with a big amethyst as a reward for his work with the Irene Adler papers. Something is incongruous here. One can understand Holmes accepting nothing but a photograph of Adler as a reward on principle, but he wouldn't change his mind and take a bejeweled gold snuffbox a few short months later unless some unrecorded event occurred to change his mind about the case and whether or not he deserved a valuable reward.

Another point to consider is the leftover expenses. At the beginning of the case, the King gives Holmes "three hundred pounds in gold and seven hundred in notes." A thousand pounds at that time is the equivalent of well over a hundred thousand pounds in the early twenty-first century. Holmes surely could not have spent a small fortune on the case, not when other than hiring a throng of paid actors outside Adler's home, he had few real expenses other than his costumes as a drunken groom and a kindly clergyman, both of which he probably already had in his possession, as well as the makeup. Neither required expensive clothes, either. Ultimately, it would be surprising if Holmes spent more than a hundred pounds on his brief investigation. Holmes gave the King a receipt, but there's no mention of Holmes returning the excess. Was he allowed to keep the incredibly large amount of change? It isn't clear, and it's surprising that Holmes doesn't mention that the King is going to get a substantial refund.

Indeed, Holmes is behaving particularly brusquely in this final scene. Traditionally, his curtness to the King is attributed to the psychological body blow caused by Holmes realizing he has been bested by Adler, which wounds not only his professional pride, but his male ego as well. That could make sense. We almost never see Holmes utterly defeated again, so it's not surprising his behavior seems uncharacteristic. Holmes isn't a good loser because he isn't accustomed to not coming out on top.

But something doesn't gel with Holmes' words and actions. It would make sense if his anger was directed towards Adler. Yet from the time he finishes reading the letter, his hostility seems to be more towards the King than Adler. Holmes asks for Adler's photograph as a memento, and from Watson's comments, he does not specifically use her image as a check on his vanity, as he uses the word "Norbury" in "The Yellow Face." Rather, he has a quiet (possibly begrudging, possibly not) respect for her. Readers can debate whether there's bitterness, admiration, resentment, attraction, or a combination of all of the above there.

In contrast, Holmes' treatment of the King is much more negative. He coldly implies that Adler is on a higher plane that the King, he rejects the precious ring (when he could easily have asked for both the photo and the ring), and refuses to shake the King's hand. Does he blame the King for leading him into a situation that led to failure? While Adler speaks briefly negatively of the King in her letter, there's nothing sufficiently passionate or revelatory to shift Holmes' opinion of the King at all.

Was Holmes a sore loser? He could have been. That leads us to reconsider all of the issues, problems, and inconsistencies throughout the stories. We have two ways to view this tale. Was Holmes playing a very long game, with a hidden agenda, and striving towards goals that went completely overlooked by Watson? Or had the great detective become so overconfident in his own powers that he completely missed gaping holes in his plans, made silly blunders that torpedoed his own best efforts, and ultimately shot his own investigation to hell? We can take an even darker view of Holmes' performance, noting that his errors may be based not just on cockiness, but on his abuse of cocaine. Watson makes a point of discussing Holmes' drug binges in the early portions of "A Scandal in Bohemia."

Yet in the opening scenes of the story, Holmes is in peak form, making shrewd observations and brilliant deductions on Watson's personal life and the identity of his coming visitor based on a piece of stationery. And considering how well Holmes gathers intelligence on Adler and organizes a plan to find the materials, it seems like we're definitely not dealing with a puffed-up popinjay whose ego exceeds his capabilities, or a strung-out junkie whose common sense has been seriously damaged. If we take "A Scandal in Bohemia" at face value, we are forced to read it as the story of a man who performs brilliantly 98% of the time, only making a couple of ridiculously puerile errors that a child would know to avoid, thereby ruining all of his efforts. I am therefore forced to conclude that Holmes did in fact deliberately throw the case of "A Scandal in Bohemia," though before explaining why this must be so, I must explain why the alternative reasons for Holmes' poor performance have to be dismissed.

How Competent Was Holmes During this Period of His Career?

There is a well-reported incident that Sir Arthur Conan Doyle once came across a man he'd never met before who claimed that in his opinion, Holmes was never the same man that he was before he faked his death. But is that the case? A careful comparison of the cases pre- and post-Reichenbach indicates that Holmes made fewer mistakes and slips after his return from the dead than he did in the earlier portion of his career. Holmes makes hardly any notable errors or lapse in judgement over the course of his later years, though he makes a few significant mistakes in the years prior to his supposed disappearance at Reichenbach Falls.

Aside from "A Scandal in Bohemia," Holmes' most famous error in a case is in "The Yellow Face," where he deduces blackmail when in fact a completely innocent personal drama is unfolding. Luckily, no harm and a great deal of good comes from the case's resolution and all ends happily. Unfortunately, there are other cases where Holmes makes a similar lapse of judgment, leading to disaster.

In addition to "A Scandal in Bohemia," there's at least one more instance in *The Adventures of Sherlock Holmes* where Holmes acts under the erroneous belief that his client's enemies won't act until he's ready. In "The Five Orange Pips," Holmes allows a client to go out into the night, where he is murdered. Holmes is deeply distraught, and his distress is not tempered by the fact that Holmes could have saved his client's life by asking him to stay at 221B until he manages to capture the villains, as other Sherlockian scholars have noted.

Comparatively, in "Silver Blaze," Holmes notes Watson's habit on focusing on Holmes' career at its best. When Watson asks why Holmes didn't travel to investigate the horse's disappearance a day earlier, Holmes replies:

> *"Because I made a blunder, my dear Watson – which is, I am afraid, a more common occurrence than anyone would think who only knew me through your memoirs. The fact is that I could not believe*

it possible that the most remarkable horse in England could long remain concealed, especially in so sparsely inhabited a place as the north of Dartmoor. From hour to hour yesterday I expected to hear that he had been found, and that his abductor was the murderer of John Straker. When, however, another morning had come and I found that beyond the arrest of young Fitzroy Simpson nothing had been done, I felt that it was time for me to take action."

Holmes' day's delay does not affect the outcome of the case, and all ends well for the horse and all connected with him. He may have judged himself as guilty of "blundering" earlier, but overall the case was solved sufficiently skillfully to be judged a rousing success.

Holmes is not perfect, as the great detective is one of the first to note. There may be many other mistakes both large and small that have escaped the public's notice due to Watson's deliberate choice to focus on the triumphs rather than the tragedies. So why would "A Scandal in Bohemia" be given a place of prominence? Holmes could not bring every case to a satisfactory conclusion, but the fact remains that his overall record was overwhelmingly filled with a string of unqualified successes. Holmes was clearly extremely competent, which makes his failure due to his own inaction and loose lips all the more striking. Was it overconfidence or underestimating the abilities of a woman that led to this pair of lapses? Could cocaine use have harmed his skills? Or was Holmes in fact demonstrating extreme competence, when he was playing for stakes that went beyond the peccadilloes of a central European monarch?

Was Holmes Ever Really a Cocaine User?

Many great heroes have serious flaws. Holmes may be a stellar detective, but no one would ever mistake him for a perfect human being. Holmes is brilliant, but he can be cold and rude, and for someone who can be so perceptive as to people's backgrounds from a few subtle physical hints, Holmes can be utterly clueless as to how his actions affect other people. But from *The Sign of Four* to "The Final Problem," there is one habit of Holmes that stands out above all others in terms of dangerousness to himself and the concern and anguish it puts on his closest friend: his drug use.

Holmes is a man who cannot stand to be bored. In the opening scene of *The Sign of Four*, after Watson begs his friend to consider the physiological and psychological toll of cocaine and morphine abuse, Holmes replies:

> *"My mind... rebels at stagnation. Give me problems, give me work, give me the most abstruse cryptogram or the most intricate analysis, and I am in my own proper atmosphere. I can dispense then with artificial stimulants. But I*

abhor the dull routine of existence. I crave for mental exaltation. That is why I have chosen my own particular profession, or rather created it, for I am the only one in the world."

It is for this reason that he turns to cocaine. The injections distract his mind from ennui. If he only had a constant stream of problems worthy of his intellect, he could pour his seven-per-cent solution of cocaine down the sink. As it is, he chooses to get high between cases.

But as anyone familiar with a compiled timeline of Holmes' cases, such as the widely consulted Baring-Gould timeline, it becomes obvious that Holmes *did* have an unending series of problems to occupy his mind from at least January of 1888 to May of 1891, and quite possibly during 1887 and even earlier: the criminal syndicate run by Prof. Moriarty. Chronologically, we know that Holmes committed himself to bringing down Moriarty's gang as early as January in 1888 in *The Valley of Fear*, featuring the first (chronologically speaking, not in terms of publication) mention of Moriarty. Given the fact that Holmes demonstrates some substantial knowledge of Moriarty's gang at this time, it can be inferred that he has been aware of Moriarty for months and even years. Though Watson is unaware of it until "The Final Problem," Holmes has devoted at minimum of three and a third years to unravelling Moriarty's web of crime. This is no simple undertaking. Holmes is undoing Moriarty's work largely single-handedly (though it's implied that at the very least, his brother Mycroft may be helping at certain points). But even if Holmes had the whole of Scotland Yard assisting him against Moriarty, the fact remains that during the aforementioned period, Holmes did have a crucial puzzle to occupy him at all times, one far more challenging than "the most abstruse cryptogram." This was the greatest problem of his life – crafting the downfall of Moriarty and his henchmen. Not an hour went by during this time when Holmes didn't have a puzzle to investigate. Indeed, Holmes knew that if he ever lost focus or abandoned this project– such as by going on a week-long drug-fueled bender – innocent people could die as a result of his negligence. Holmes therefore had no reason to be bored, and had an additional moral duty to refrain from crippling himself with drug use. Why then, would he turn to the hypodermic needle so frequently?

The most obvious and convincing answer is that he didn't. Sherlock Holmes was not a drug user. He most likely injected himself with plain water on multiple occasions in front of Watson, knowing that his friend would report these actions, and tell the entire world through his tales that Holmes routinely addled himself with cocaine. As shown in "The Dying Detective," Holmes could fool his medically trained friend. With the right chemical in his eyes to mimic the effects of drug use, and by mimicking the effects of a cocaine binge through skillful acting, it's conceivable that Watson could have been misled into believing that Holmes really was getting high.

But why, a hypothetical questioner might ask, would Holmes create the impression that he was a drug addict? Why would a man who required a sterling reputation allow drug use to taint it? Holmes was required to give testimony in court on multiple occasions. How could he risk a dangerous criminal being set free if the defense counsel could convincingly posit that his judgment and observations were critically impaired from the use of cocaine?

The answer is simple. Holmes conducted this elaborate charade for the primary purpose of convincing Moriarty that he had a mammoth Achilles' heel in addiction.

It is an effective ploy – gain an advantage over an enemy by leading your opponent to believe that you are weaker than you actually are. Many famous detectives have adopted a pose of appearing foolish or ridiculous for the purpose of getting others to underestimate them. Columbo is famous for appearing disheveled and blundering, all to put the targets of his homicide investigations off their guard. Hercule Poirot plays up the role of the flamboyant mountebank in order to trick insular Britons into thinking that a comic Belgian cannot solve crimes. Father Brown's cherubic innocence fools criminals into believing that he cannot possibly comprehend the evils that men can do. What could be a more natural way for Holmes to handicap himself in the eyes of a brilliant adversary than to create the impression that he suffers from an addiction that impairs his judgement at inopportune times?

It is an effective ploy. Holmes' existing reputation means that he cannot present himself as a bungler or a fool, but he could exhibit a purported fondness for cocaine.

Perhaps the most telling evidence that Holmes' cocaine usage was a feint comes from the stories taking place after the confrontation with Moriarty at Reichenbach Falls. It has been often noted that Holmes' cocaine (and morphine, for that matter) habit ceased upon his return in "The Empty House." Many Sherlockian scholars have noted this, and some think that he cured himself of this habit during the time he pretended to be dead. Nicholas Meyer's novel *The Seven-Per-Cent Solution* uses this as its premise, having Holmes being forced to seek treatment for his addiction at the hands of no less an authority than Sigmund Freud himself, before embarking on the Great Hiatus for reasons other than the ones noted in the original Canon. But it's remarkable that even if a heavy cocaine user were able to completely kick the habit, that Holmes never shows any indication of wishing to relapse.

Addiction rarely works that way. With assistance, treatment, and support, a recovering addict may never take drugs again, but the desire to resume the habit almost always remains to some degree. This was a critical plot point of the television series *Elementary*, where Holmes was in a constant battle to maintain his sobriety. It is notable that Watson, who makes a point of depicting all of the details, never mentions Holmes showing the faintest hint of a craving for cocaine or the slightest sign of an impending relapse. Indeed, Holmes eventually retires, and spends extended periods of times occupying his mind and time primarily with beekeeping-related issues, never turning to artificial stimulants to activate his mind. While it is possible that Holmes' mental temperament might have changed with age, unfortunately, cocaine addicts tend to wrestle with the urge to relapse for the rest of their lives. The fact that Holmes shows no yearning whatsoever to return to the drug is highly suspicious. He does not show any signs that he is still suffering from the scars of addiction, which sadly, in the vast majority of addiction cases, never fully heal.

Cocaine also plays only a very small role in the pre-Reichenbach stories. The word "cocaine" only appears nine times in the Canon, and five of these references are in *The Sign of Four,* four times in the opening scene where Holmes' drug use is first discussed, and once in the closing line of the book. Of the remaining four instances, three of them are only fleeting references to Holmes using the drug on occasion in the past. The only time we ever hear of Holmes taking the drug for extended binges for a long period of time is in the opening of "A Scandal in Bohemia."

Given the very minor role that this very addictive drug really played in Holmes' life, and for all the reasons listed above, a strong argument can be advanced that Holmes simply feigned drug use and cocaine benders in front of Watson, who dutifully included these details in his "warts and all" depiction of his friend. But it was all a clever misinformation campaign, a ruse of Holmes' to convince Moriarty that the great detective suffered from nonexistent flaws that the professor could exploit.

The Mysterious Marriage[*]

Anybody who has a rudimentary knowledge of English marriage law during the late nineteenth century and the religious rituals of marriage realizes that something is very wrong with Irene Adler's marriage. Some Sherlockian scholars have suggested that Holmes' account of the wedding of Adler and Norton is flawed or distorted, but why would Holmes feed such a deeply flawed story to his friend? What could he possibly gain at this time by suggesting that there was something fishy about Adler's marriage? There is a much darker and probable possibility, and that is that Adler's wedding was actually a cruel and deliberate sham.

In Holmes' account of the wedding, he witnesses Norton rushing into Adler's home around eleven-thirty in the morning, where he speaks to her in a state of severe agitation before rushing out and looking flustered. Adler and Norton take off for the Church of St. Monica in the Edgeware Road in separate carriages, both promising their coachmen

[*] I am deeply grateful for Derrick Belanger and David Marcum for their assistance with the research for this chapter, and for the critically helpful annotations in the Baring-Gould, Oxford and both Klinger versions of the *Annotated Sherlock Holmes*.

extra money if they get there in twenty minutes. The reason for the different conveyances stems from the fact that Norton has to stop at Gross and Hankey's in Regent Street first – perhaps he needed to pick up the wedding rings. The rush stems from the fact that both parties are trying to get to the church by noon.

Holmes reaches St. Monica's to find Adler, Norton, and a priest there, and is surprised when Norton drags him to the altar to act as a witness. Norton promises that the wedding will last only three minutes. Holmes explains that:

> *"I was half-dragged up to the altar, and before I knew where I was I found myself mumbling responses which were whispered in my ear, and vouching for things of which I knew nothing, and generally assisting in the secure tying up of Irene Adler, spinster, to Godfrey Norton, bachelor. It was all done in an instant, and there was the gentleman thanking me on the one side and the lady on the other, while the clergyman beamed on me in front. It was the most preposterous*

position in which I ever found myself in my life, and it was the thought of it that started me laughing just now. It seems that there had been some informality about their license, that the clergyman absolutely refused to marry them without a witness of some sort, and that my lucky appearance saved the bridegroom from having to sally out into the streets in search of a best man. The bride gave me a sovereign, and I mean to wear it on my watch-chain in memory of the occasion."

Immediately after the wedding, Adler and Norton go their separate ways, and Adler declares that she will go out for her usual five p.m. carriage ride. Holmes returned to Baker Street and recounted his recent experiences to Watson.

The problem is, there are a lot of eyebrow-raising details that give rise to serious concerns about the validity of the wedding. Norton spoke of an informality about the license, but at that time, no license could be so informal that most of the standard rules and procedures of a wedding ceremony could be thrown out the stained-glass window.

Though the geography of the Holmesian universe does not always match the London we know today, it should be noted that there is no Church of St. Monica in the Edgeware Road. Today, there is a St. Monica's Church in Palmers Green, London, and St. Monica's Priory in Hoxton. Both are Catholic churches. If we ignore the Edgeware Road and focus on the St. Monica's portion (perhaps Watson misheard or misremembered "Edgeware" for "Stonard," the true road where the Palmers Green St. Monica's is located), then that means that the wedding took place in a Catholic church. This implies that Adler, and most likely Norton as well, were Catholics. If one of them was not a Catholic, they would have to be married in the rectory rather than the church itself. Alternatively, if Watson recorded the name of the church incorrectly, then they might well have been married in an Anglican ceremony. The question over whether the ceremony was a Catholic or Protestant one will be an important point as we look over Holmes' account of the wedding.

The first issue when reading "A Scandal in Bohemia" that might mystify some readers is the rush to get to the church. One would think that if the pair had planned their wedding well ahead of time that they would have had time to draw up their schedules to allow plenty of time to get to the church without having to rush so desperately. It's notable that neither party had any close friends nor relatives invited to the wedding, and that they came to the church individually. Possibly they took off in separate carriages so Adler could assure the priest that the groom was on his way, and only needed to pick up the rings.

Contemporary readers might not understand the urgency to get married before noon, and the mad rush may make current readers think only of the song from *My Fair Lady* "Get Me to the Church on Time." The historical context of the day needs to be put into place. Up until May 1886, there was a law in England that required weddings to take place in the morning, with noon being the cutoff time. This partially explains why Norton was in such a rush. If they were to get married that day, then they had to get themselves to the church with enough time before noon for the ceremony to be completed. But that begs another question – why was it so important that they get married that day? Why couldn't they wait until another day to take their vows? What issue got Norton so worked up that he could not possibly have gone without being married to Adler for another day, and the reasons for his excitement were so compelling that Adler agreed that she would get married at once? Those questions will be addressed later.

Going back to the historical laws at the time, the May 1886 law changed the marriage deadline to three in the afternoon, though this was directed solely towards Church of England marriages, and did not affect Catholic weddings. In today's world, where anybody can become an "ordained minister" by going online, and marriages can take place anytime, anywhere, it may be surprising for present-day readers to learn that there were rules against late afternoon and evening marriages at this time. During the late nineteenth century, there were special licenses that removed all time restrictions, though special circumstances or influence were often needed to get them, generally from the Archbishop of Canterbury himself for Anglicans.

In both Anglican and Catholic practices, the banns– an announcement of marriage– were put up well before the ceremony in order to have time for objections to the wedding to be raised. The absence of banns might not affect the legality of an Anglican marriage under special license, though the situation was more questionable for a Catholic marriage.

When Holmes arrived at the church, according to his description, there were only three people there. The fact that the clergyman there was referred to as a "priest" does not prove the religion of the church, as both Catholics and Anglicans use the term "priest," though this title and the fact that the church is named for a saint rule out many (though not all) other Protestant denominations. Holmes was then dragged to the altar to serve as a witness. Notably, no one else besides the bride, groom, and the priest is mentioned, and this is bizarre, as weddings required two witnesses for validity. There was a coachman waiting outside, and any other stranger could do, but the disguised Holmes was the sole witness. Why wasn't a second witness brought in for the ceremony?

It seems very odd that Norton, a lawyer, would allow himself to get married with only half the required witnesses.

Not only that, but in Anglican weddings at this time, the witnesses do not have to "mumble responses" or "vouch for things." Signing their names to a register is all they have to do. In Latin rite Catholic ceremonies at the time, there was a need for responses to Latin questions and prayers. Given this situation, and Holmes' obvious confusion possibly being exacerbated by Latin, this seems to be the strongest evidence yet the ceremony took place in a Catholic church.

The length of the ceremony raises another question mark. Catholic and Anglican wedding ceremonies at this time are generally much longer affairs, often performed as part of a Mass for Catholics. It was not simply a matter of saying "Do you? Do you? You're married!" Even the most rapidly speaking clergyman would find it impossible to perform a valid wedding ceremony "in an instant," as Holmes says.

The idea of an "informality about the license" is also eyebrow-raising. In certain circumstances clergymen could dispense with the standard rules and the marriage would remain perfectly legal, but with all of these questionable actions and shady omissions, all performed under the oversight of a seemingly respectable lawyer, it all seems very unusual, as if there's some deliberate attempt to render the marriage invalid.

Indeed, Norton's behavior seems extremely odd. He rushes to his paramour's house in the late morning in a state of agitation, convinces Adler to marry him immediately, and then performs a string of actions that raises doubt about the validity of the wedding. It's almost as if he didn't want to be legally married to Irene Adler at all...

Is Irene Adler Alive or Dead?

What happened to Irene Adler after the events of "A Scandal in Bohemia"? Sherlockian scholars have long debated whether she is alive or dead, largely based on Watson's line early in the story, calling her "the late Irene Adler."

Some people interpret this as meaning that Adler is deceased, but others point out that the "late" may simply refer to that being her former name, and that she now goes by her married name, Mrs. Irene Norton. Some Sherlockians insist that Adler is deceased, and come up with some shocking theories as to how she met her demise.

However, the Canon provides one solid indicator that she is still alive. The most telling – and convincing – evidence that Irene Adler is not actually dead comes in "The Last Bow," when Holmes says, "It was I who brought about the separation between Irene Adler and the late King of Bohemia when your cousin Heinrich was the Imperial Envoy." If we interpret "late" to mean "deceased," rather than the alternative usage of the word to mean "abdicated," then why wouldn't Holmes refer to "the late Irene Adler" as well? Holmes would likely be consistent, especially when showing honor to a deceased woman whom he respected. In this context, it sounds as if Adler is still alive, and the King is dead, or has possibly abdicated. If this is so, then Watson simply meant "the former" when he referred to Adler as "late."

There is one alternative explanation for Watson referring to "the late Irene Adler." What if Watson genuinely believed that Adler were dead at the time that he wrote his account of the case, when in fact she was still alive, and Holmes knew that in 1914? It's an intriguing possibility that leads to some interesting speculation.

What Happened to the King of Bohemia?

After Holmes snubbed the King of Bohemia and left Irene Adler's abandoned home, what happened to the King of Bohemia? Did he return to his home country, announce his engagement, marry, and reign relatively peacefully and with minimal scandal? Unlike most of Holmes' cases, "A Scandal in Bohemia" is referenced several times in later tales, and these brief mentions provide some intriguing glimpses at the future of the Bohemian monarch.

In "A Case of Identity," which the Baring-Gould timeline places at five months after "A Scandal in Bohemia," Holmes and Watson have the following exchange:

> *"He held out his snuffbox of old gold, with a great amethyst in the centre of the lid. Its splendour was in such contrast to his homely ways and simple life that I could not help commenting upon it.*
>
> *"Ah," said he, "I forgot that I had not seen you for some weeks. It is a little souvenir from the King of Bohemia in*

return for my assistance in the case of the Irene Adler papers."

"And the ring?" I asked, glancing at a remarkable brilliant which sparkled upon his finger.

"It was from the reigning family of Holland, though the matter in which I served them was of such delicacy that I cannot confide it even to you, who have been good enough to chronicle one or two of my little problems.""

Holmes' proud display of this valuable trinket is confusing, given his behavior in "A Scandal in Bohemia." Holmes made a point of not only preferring Adler's picture to an emerald snake ring proffered by the King (surely, if Holmes were claiming a reward, he could have easily asked for and received both!), but also failing to shake the King's hand, though whether this was a deliberate snub or a result of Holmes being distracted by his consternation and bruised ego is open to debate. Yet as "A Case of Identity" shows, Holmes has now accepted a marvelous and valuable gift from the King of Bohemia, and the gold and amethyst snuffbox is now prominently displayed in his rooms. Either Holmes' opinion of the King and the case changed dramatically, or there is something else at play here. It is clear that Holmes did not refuse the emerald snake ring out of an aversion to jewelry, as the bauble from the Royal Family of Holland indicates.

Later in "A Case of Identity," Watson comments that the Adler/King of Bohemia case is the one and only time that he has known Holmes to fail. "The Blue Carbuncle" contains a brief mention of the Adler case as a recent investigation that was not about solving an actual crime. In "The Copper Beeches," there is a passing reference to "A Scandal in Bohemia," where Holmes again remarks on how some of his cases do not deal with situations that are legally crimes, and lists four such cases from *The Adventures of Sherlock Holmes*, including "The small matter in which I endeavoured to help the King of Bohemia." This is an interesting choice of words, as a scandal with the potential to break up an arranged royal wedding, and potentially bring down a monarch, is referred to as a "small matter."

But the most notable reference to "A Scandal in Bohemia" comes in the last Holmes tale, in a chronological sense. In "His Last Bow," Holmes taunts the captured German spy Heinrich Von Bork, informing him that "It was I who brought about the separation between Irene Adler and the late King of Bohemia when your cousin Heinrich was the Imperial Envoy." "His Last Bow" is set in 1914. That means, between "A Scandal in Bohemia" in 1887 and the start of WWI, the King of Bohemia either passed away – the manner of his death being unknown – or he abdicated, and the word "late" simply means "former" in this context. Either way, the man introduced in "A Scandal in Bohemia" no longer wears the country's crown. Upon reflection, an abdication, except in cases of advanced age or illness, invariably brings a scandal that a nation's government does not need, so the King's fate is more likely, though not definitely, to be death.

But how long has the King of Bohemia, Wilhelm Gottsreich Sigismond von Ormstein, Grand Duke of Cassel-Felstein, been off the throne?

There's no direct evidence as to whether he has been gone for days or decades. Based on the confusing matter of the declined emerald snake ring and the accepted gold and amethyst snuffbox, there's a possibility that Holmes did not simply change his mind about accepting a bejeweled memento from the King of Bohemia as a token of thanks for his services in the Adler case. A period of some months has passed between "A Scandal in Bohemia" and "A Case of Identity." Is it possible, that the King of Bohemia who offered the ring and the King who sent the snuffbox are two different monarchs? Could Wilhelm Gottsreich Sigismond von Ormstein have died soon after the events of "A Scandal in Bohemia," and a man whom Holmes respected more have been coronated? And could the Adler scandal have still been potentially inflammatory, leading to continued investigation on Holmes' part? These are definite possibilities.

Did Holmes Break Up Irene Adler and the King?

Holmes knew of Irene Adler and her relationship with the King of Bohemia before the events of "A Scandal in Bohemia." Early in the story, Holmes reveals that he has information about the two of them in his personal files:

> *"The facts are briefly these: Some five years ago, during a lengthy visit to Warsaw, I made the acquaintance of the well-known adventuress, Irene Adler. The name is no doubt familiar to you."*

> *"Kindly look her up in my index, Doctor," murmured Holmes without opening his eyes. For many years he had adopted a system of docketing all paragraphs concerning men and things, so that it was difficult to name a subject or a person on which he could not at once furnish information. In this case I found her biography sandwiched in between that of a Hebrew rabbi and that of a staff-commander who had written a monograph upon the deep-sea fishes.*

"Let me see!" said Holmes. "Hum! Born in New Jersey in the year 1858. Contralto–hum! La Scala, hum! Prima donna Imperial Opera of Warsaw–yes! Retired from operatic stage–ha! Living in London–quite so! Your Majesty, as I understand, became entangled with this young person, wrote her some compromising letters, and is now desirous of getting those letters back."

"Precisely so. But how– –"

How indeed? How did Holmes know so much about the King's affair with Adler? The relationship between the King and Adler could not have been in the tabloids or even been the subject of much gossip, otherwise Holmes would know that the Scandinavian Royal Family was almost certainly already aware of the liaison, which means that the King's excuse for needing to cover up the relationship would not hold water. As a prominent singer, Adler was a minor celebrity, so it is not surprising that the King might expect that Holmes would have known about her existence. What is shocking is the fact that Holmes' files contain information about the incriminating letters. As the King explains, this is a matter so delicate that he dares not share it with anyone else. Secrets like this have a habit of leaking. How is it that Holmes could possess such delicate information?

It seems likely that Holmes was fully aware of the King's relationship with Irene Adler for years, and evidence to support this view comes much later in the Canon's chronology. To reiterate, a brief line in "His Last Bow" has Holmes reveal that he was instrumental in severing the Adler/King relationship when he informs a German spymaster, "It was I who brought about the separation between Irene Adler and the late King of Bohemia when your cousin Heinrich was the Imperial Envoy." If we accept this statement as true, and that the "separation" refers to the initial breakup between the pair, then Holmes knew the secret details behind the relationship for years, and someone, unbeknownst to the King and Adler, hired Holmes to destroy the liaison. Who and why are not revealed in the Canon, so we are left with only speculation. The revelation that "A Scandal in

Bohemia" is not the first time that the King and Adler have been the subject of one of Holmes' adventures is thought-provoking, and perhaps sheds an entirely different light on Holmes accepting the case from the King. The potential reasons for Holmes getting involved in the breakup will be explored later in this monograph.

Incidentally, Watson may have committed an inadvertent security breach by revealing this brief glimpse into the context of Holmes' index. By mentioning the fact that in at least one instance, potentially inflammatory secrets were tucked away in Holmes' records, Watson might have inspired some blackmail-minded ruffian to break into 221B while it was unoccupied and rummage through the files in search of information that could be parlayed into cash. The accounts of top-secret cases that Watson keeps in a battered tin dispatch-box are at least safe in a bank vault, but 221B unfortunately does not enjoy that level of security.

The fact that Adler is included in Holmes' index takes on an added level of interest when we remember from *A Study in Scarlet* that Holmes believes in collecting only information that he deems of use to him. Watson may have created the false impression that Holmes had created a veritable *Who's Who* of everything in his files, but if Holmes were to continuously update his records with everything of note, he would have no time for anything else. It seems more in keeping with Holmes' character and schedule that he would only keep records on people connected to his cases.

When Holmes accepted the case to break up Adler and the King, did he know all of the details of the sensitive nature of their relationship? His comment that shows that he did not know that both parties were included in the photograph, it is clear that certain details about relationship were withheld from Holmes. Holmes may not have known the full details of the King and Adler's romance, but he must have believed whoever hired him and that severing the pair was in the cause of some greater good. Little is known for certain, but it can be inferred that the person who asked Holmes to destroy Adler and the King's relationship never dreamt that Adler might try to use the papers in her position to get revenge on the King and prevent his future marriage, or else Holmes' unknown client would have asked Holmes to get ahold of all the incriminating documents at the time he destroyed their relationship.

The King and the Professor

While there is no direct evidence in the Canon that the King of Bohemia and Professor Moriarty were ever acquainted, I believe that the deductions and influences of the previous chapters justify the extension of this theory, which will be expanded upon in the following sketch. Let us suppose, that since there is good reason to suspect that the King of Bohemia was under the sway of a powerful and malevolent figure, and that Moriarty was the only known criminal figure of this stature in the Canon, that Moriarty was indeed controlling the King.

We will never know exactly how Moriarty gained power over the King. Perhaps the King's lustful escapades left him vulnerable to blackmail. Maybe the King needed money, and joined forces with the Professor to gain those funds. There is even the possibility that some really dark, nasty secret in the King's past led to his recruitment into Moriarty's gang. Whatever happened, the King found himself in an unprecedented situation, where an obscure academic now held the power to compel a monarch to do his bidding!

What follows is pure speculation, but it answers the questions that have been identified in the earlier chapters of this monograph.

Moriarty and the King

(The night of Saturday, May 21ˢᵗ, 1887. The scene is The KING's suite at the Langham luxury hotel in London. There is the sound of a key in the lock, and after a moment the KING OF BOHEMIA enters the room. He switches on the light and shuts the door. He does not notice a figure emerging from the shadows.)

MORIARTY. Good evening, Your Majesty. *(There is a faint mocking tone in "Majesty.")*

KING. *(Jumps, and whirls around.)* Professor! What are you doing here!

MORIARTY. Come, come, your Majesty, surely that is obvious. I want to know what progress you have made in retrieving the photograph.

KING. I can assure you that the situation is under control.

MORIARTY. *(Steps forward.)* You will forgive me for my skepticism, but I believe that I am justified in doubting your confidence. After all, I tasked you with retrieving the photograph months ago. You have made numerous attempts to retrieve it, and each one has failed. Why should I believe that this new attempt will be successful? Just because you hired Sherlock Holmes?

KING. *(Stunned.)* How did you know?

MORIARTY. There is little that occurs in London without my knowledge. I dare say that I know your movements over the past year better than you do. In all honesty, I think that you've finally found a competent person to retrieve the photograph.

KING. You know Holmes?

MORIARTY. We've never met, but he's crossed my path. He's a clever man, but not nearly so astute as he thinks he is. He believes that he can bring me down, which just goes to show that he overestimates his own abilities.

KING. Do you think he'll fail?

MORIARTY. On the contrary, I think it's very likely that he'll succeed. Which makes the situation even more dangerous. You've probably hired one of the very few men in London who can help you retrieve the photograph from Miss Adler, and also one who must not see that photograph at any cost.

KING. Was I wrong to turn to him?

MORIARTY. More likely than not, he'll find the photograph. And then he'll look at it, and then he'll know about my connection to you. *(Leans forward, suddenly angry.)* I have no interest in dictating to you how you ought to live your personal life. Your relationship to Irene Adler is of no significance whatsoever to me. But you allowed yourself to be photographed at your residence with her...

KING. But Professor, how could I possibly have known that you would be arriving to visit me at that moment? When the photographer took the picture of us, there was no way I could possibly have known that you were walking down the street at that moment–

MORIARTY. Nevertheless, I was! And now, my profile is clearly visible through the window in that wretched photograph. That superannuated singer thinks that the danger in the photograph comes from the fact that you both appear in it. Luckily, she has no idea that it's dangerous because it shows that I was visiting you in Bohemia. And you know that we cannot afford for there to be any public knowledge that the two of us are acquainted. The situation is far too delicate. I go to extraordinary lengths to keep myself as anonymous as possible. If Holmes gets ahold of that picture, his beady little eyes will notice me immediately, and then he'll realize at once that I have a stake in Bohemian affairs.

KING. He hasn't seen it yet! He's found the photograph, but he hasn't taken it.

MORIARTY. What? Why not? If he knows where it is, why hasn't he stolen it yet?

KING. I don't know. He just says that I'm to join him tomorrow to retrieve it.

MORIARTY. I see. That's very obliging of him.

KING. What do you mean?

MORIARTY. Simply put, it's possible that we may be able to retrieve that photograph without any attention-grabbing bloodshed.

KING. *(Blanches.)* Bloodshed?

MORIARTY. Of course. If Holmes picks up the picture and sees me, and if there's a scene when Miss Adler enters the room, you'll have to act quickly. I presume you keep your revolver fully loaded?

KING. *(Pats his shoulder holster nervously.)* Of course. But you can't possibly expect me to use it!

MORIARTY. Of course I do! If Adler causes a confrontation, and if there's no way to take the photograph peacefully, I expect you to take out your revolver and fire until there are no more witnesses! Holmes, Adler, her servants, even that doctor friend of Holmes' if he joins you. Then, take the photograph and hurry back here as soon as possible.

KING. But it'll be a massacre!

MORIARTY. Yes, but before the simpletons at Scotland Yard start investigating, you'll be on your way home to Bohemia, and my agents will have covered your tracks.

KING. I can't! I'm not a mass murderer!

MORIARTY. *(Leans forward.)* I know you, Your Majesty, and I know you are no innocent. I have no doubt that you can bring yourself to take multiple lives if your well-being is at stake. But comfort yourself, for it is more likely than not you won't have to go to such extremes. It's possible that you'll be able to snatch the photograph before Holmes gets a chance to look at it. In that case, you can pocket it and be gone, and there's no need for bloodshed. But in the event that Holmes gets a glimpse of the photograph, then you'll have to assume that he sees me in the picture and has started making those dratted deductions he's so famous for crafting. If that happens, then you'll have to take steps, but a bit more subtly this time. *(Pulls a little box out of his pocket.)*

KING. What's that?

MORIARTY. *(Opens the box.)* A piece of jewelry for you, your Majesty. A snake ring. Try it on, but be very careful with it.

KING. Why?

MORIARTY. Like many snake rings, it contains poison. Press the emerald, and a tiny pair of fangs will protrude from the snake's mouth, and if they pierce Holmes' skin, they'll inject a solution of concentrated cocaine into his bloodstream.

KING. Cocaine?

MORIARTY. Yes. They'll find him in his rooms several hours later, and they'll examine him, and assume that he died of an overdose. His best friend will attest to his drug use. He simply took too much, and so, farewell Mr. Holmes!

KING. You want me to kill Sherlock Holmes?

MORIARTY. *(Testily.)* That is what I said. Don't waste my time repeating everything I tell you. You know, upon further reflection, no matter what happens, I think that Mr. Holmes has gotten too close for comfort for me. Even if he doesn't see the photograph, offer him this ring as a reward. And then, as you slip it on his finger, trigger the poison fangs so they pierce the neighboring finger. They're very thin, he'll feel nothing, a tiny twinge at most. Then make a hasty retreat. You won't have to watch him die, and when Holmes is cooling on a slab at the morgue, one of my minions will retrieve the ring.

KING. Why must I do this?

MORIARTY. Because you made a foolish mistake. It was your photograph that left me exposed. Your last several attempts failed. Come to think of it, I have no reason to trust you to succeed now. Upon further reflection, I'm going to send a team to search Adler's house during the night. If the photograph is in her house, I don't want it out of my possession for a minute less than necessary, and I don't trust you to retrieve it safely. You may not have to meet Holmes tomorrow after all, so you'd better hope they find the photograph. But if they don't, then you'll have to pay for your mistake with the blood of others.

KING. But...

MORIARTY. If you'd retrieved the photograph months ago, when I learned of its existence from my spies and asked you to get it for me, you'd never have brought Sherlock Holmes into this matter in the first place. This is your fault, and now you must pay the price. Retrieve the photograph and kill Sherlock Holmes, or face the consequences. *(Walks towards the door.)*

KING. You cannot threaten me! I am the King of Bohemia!

MORIARTY. True. But I... am Professor Moriarty. Do as you're told, Your Majesty. *(Exits.)*

> *(The KING shakes, and crumples into a chair.)*
> *(End of scene.)*

I make no claims that this is a word-for-word account of an actual conversation, but it mirrors the messages that must have been shared. It answers most of the nagging questions I addressed earlier in this monograph.

First of all, the significance of the photograph. Once again, the photograph was actually no more dangerous than the letters Holmes observed could be discredited. Likewise, a look-alike for the King or photographic manipulation could explain away the picture. This theory of events provides a reason why the King would want to obtain the photograph– because the potentially damaging imagery captured isn't of the King and Adler, but of Professor Moriarty, who didn't realize he was being photographed at a place he didn't wish people to know he visited. The need for the cover-up explains the King's lies and lapses in logic.

Second, the ransacking of Adler's home. Holmes had no reason to order it. If the King trusted Holmes' judgment as he claimed, the King would have had no need to search for the photograph. Even though Adler was in a hurry, she wasn't in such a terrible rush that she had to tear the room apart to gather the items she wanted. Perhaps she might have left some drawers open, but she wouldn't have had to dismantle the shelves or drag the furniture around the room. Logically, some other party with both the knowledge and the desire for the photograph had to have been involved, someone who wasn't willing to wait several hours, who didn't know where the photograph was located and weren't clever enough to find the hidden panel, and who wasn't afraid if the noise being made from turning the room upside-down woke up anybody. This last point indicates that not only were the late-night plunderers unafraid of being caught, but it can therefore be extrapolated that they were willing and able to use violence, possibly even deadly force, to make their escape.

Third, the King's state of agitation. Monarchs are not in the habit of touching commoners for more than a quick handshake if they can possibly help it, yet the King grabs Holmes by the shoulders that last morning, and looks him directly in the face. He's anxious, twitchy, and desperate to be in possession of the photograph. The King clearly still carries a torch for Adler, and either his ego or deep-seated denial, possibly both, lead him to disbelieve that she could possibly have gotten over him and instead directed her affections to some mere lawyer. His sulkiness at the news that his former lover is now wedded to someone else illustrates that his own ardor for Adler is far from dissipated. Yet despite the fact that the photograph is still a danger to him even if Adler keeps her word, he's downright enthusiastic and overjoyed upon reading the letter. Moriarty's orders to kill that I theorize explain this change of attitude. His relief isn't due to the safety of the photograph, but due to the fact that *he will no longer be called upon to kill Irene Adler, a woman he still cares about and does not wish to see harmed.* The sudden jubilation, along with the knowledge that she is fled and is in reduced danger from Moriarty, changes his mood. Having had no time to reflect upon the matter, the King assumes that Moriarty will accept that Adler will keep the photograph hidden, little realizing that Moriarty is unlikely to embrace the situation, and will surely go after Adler and the documents.

Of course, the King had no similar feelings of affection for Holmes. While he dreaded the prospect of shooting his former love, he accepted the order to poison Holmes. Not only that, but the King's state of mind was so jittery that he never thought to ask Holmes for his considerable change from the lavish expense money he'd given the detective. He didn't realize that Holmes was one step ahead of him.

This leads into the final incongruous point being discussed here: Holmes' rudeness and refusal to shake hands with the King. The theory that Holmes was simply in a state of pique after being defeated by Adler is of course possible, but the snub of a handshake from a monarch is a social offense so grave that no matter how annoyed Holmes may have been with himself, he should have been able to exert sufficient control over his emotions to give the monarch a proper farewell.

Holmes' behavior is incongruous for multiple reasons. It seems as if he deliberately sabotaged his own mission by refusing to grab the photograph when he had the opportunity and publicly discussing critical information so Adler could overhear it. Yet if he's trying to avoid a scandal as he's supposed to, why did he invite the King along with them to Adler's house? Had Adler been awake and confronted the trio, there could very well have been a major confrontation and the resulting uproar, if sufficient witnesses in the neighborhood overheard it, could have provoked a crisis sufficient to end the King's engagement, with or without the photograph.

It made no logical sense to take the King along with them. It exposed the monarch, and being seen in public with the King would indicate that he had hired Holmes for something. Holmes suggests that the King might want to retrieve the photograph himself, but surely the King would prefer maintaining his anonymity more. If there's no clear benefit having the King visit Adler's home, perhaps there's a parallel issue at play here. Suppose that the real purpose of bringing the King with them was to leave his hotel suite empty for a short period of time, allowing an ally of Holmes' to search for something of interest there! If Holmes suspected a link between the King and Moriarty, and Holmes' agent located some incriminating documents in the room, Holmes could have been alerted to this fact, possibly by some associate of his standing in the street and signaling Holmes in some way through the window.

If that's the case, and Holmes' suspicions about the King's perfidy were confirmed, that that explains the additional coldness towards the monarch. Not only did Holmes know for certain that King had an ulterior motive and was not being fully honest with him, but the ever-observant Holmes probably noticed the new snake ring (Watson hadn't mentioned the King wearing it before in his very thorough description of the monarch at their first meeting.), and Holmes' arcane knowledge of such items of jewelry, and perhaps a glimpse at the fangs on the ring told him that it was dangerous. Hence, Holmes was not being rude when he refused the ring and the handshake. He was acting out of self-preservation, preventing himself from being poisoned. Not only that, but he neglected to offer to return the extra money to the King, feeling as if under the circumstances, he'd earned a heftier fee.

There's another reason why Holmes asked for the photograph of Adler besides acknowledging her triumph over him. This was a purely practical reason – Holmes needed Adler's image. Holmes knew that Adler was still in danger, and that Moriarty would not rest until he had tracked her down and reclaimed the photograph. Holmes needed a high-quality picture of Adler to copy and send to his associates to aid them in tracking her down. Holmes knew that the case of "A Scandal in Bohemia" wasn't over yet, and it wouldn't be until he'd assured himself that Adler was safe.

It is unclear how Moriarty learned that he was in the photo, but it might have had something to do with the glass plate negative. The King might have carelessly mentioned the photograph with Adler when Moriarty met with him shortly after the picture was taken, not realizing its inflammatory nature. Years later, when the royal engagement was looming, Moriarty, several steps ahead of the King, realized that the photograph might endanger the King's position at some point in the future. One of Moriarty's henchmen could have swiped the glass plate negative from the photographer's studio archives and brought it to his boss. Imagine Moriarty's shock and horror when he saw his own face in the photo! Moriarty was at that time known only in academic circles, but if this photograph found its way into the newspapers, he could gain some deeply unwanted publicity.

A Report From the Colonel

Based on the hints in the Canon, a strong inference may be drawn that the King of Bohemia died sometime in the approximately five months between the events of "A Scandal in Bohemia" and "A Case of Identity." But how did he die? He was a fairly young man, only about thirty years of age, and in robust physical condition. Could the King have met with foul play? And if so, could it have something to do with his association with Professor Moriarty? What follows is purely speculative, but it's a possible way that the King might have met his demise in a way that would not have drawn unwanted attention or scandal.

To continue upon my previous string of inferences which led to the conclusion that the King was under Professor Moriarty's thumb, let us then continue upon the that thread and suggest that the King eventually became a liability for Moriarty. After all, a King who would allow himself to be put into a position where he could be blackmailed and manipulated is not a man who displays solid judgment. Perhaps the King was making other errors that could expose Moriarty's plans. Possibly

Moriarty never forgave him for not eliminating Holmes. Alternatively, royal monarchs are not accustomed to taking orders from criminal commoners. Perhaps the King decided to reassert his dominance, and told Moriarty to go climb a tree. The Professor could not stand for insubordination, for any show of weakness could imperil his hold over his criminal organization.

All of what follows is once again pure speculation, but we do know that if someone was standing in Moriarty's way, the Professor would not hesitate to eliminate that figure, even if that person did wear a crown. Sherlockians know from reading "The Empty House" that one of the Professor's most trusted assassins was Colonel Sebastian Moran. What if Moran were the man tasked with eliminating the King of Bohemia? If so, the Colonel's report to the Professor might have gone something like this:

•••

J.M.–

I send this message through the usual channels and utilizing the agreed-upon cipher, knowing that you will follow your own protocol regarding the destruction of this note. When you appointed me as your chief of staff, I made it clear that I would only use my talents with a rifle on the most high-class jobs, but I suppose that the assassination of a king is as high-class as can be imagined.

As you asked, I gave the King of Bohemia one last chance to make things right with you before acting. Upon arriving in Bohemia, I sent one of my most trusted men to infiltrate a state dinner. He managed to exchange a few words with the King and demand that he resume his work for you, but the King seemed to have grown a backbone since your last meeting, and he flat-out refused and ordered his guards to seize my associate. Fortunately, he managed to escape into the crowd, and I sent him back to England, now that his face was known.

I began gathering reconnaissance on the King. I started patronizing a small tavern where members of the palace staff are known to relax after a busy day of pampering a spoiled monarch. I situated myself in a corner, and pretended to be engrossed in a book. By making a great show of pretending I didn't speak or understand the local lingo and speaking only

English loudly and slowly, I was able to put the royal household employees off their guard, and they managed to provide me with some useful information as they spoke freely in front of me, convinced that I could not make heads nor tails of what they were saying. I learned that the King was being closely watched by agents of the Prime Minister, who was determined to prevent the lecherous duffer from getting involved with another unsuitable woman before the marriage to the Scandinavian princess is safely tied up. After the wedding, I'm assuming the King would have been allowed to run free again. It's not easy to control a man who thinks he ought to wield power due to divine right, as you well know. Eventually, I learned that the King was in the habit of taking long horseback rides in the countryside, and after adopting the guise of a rambler, I started to explore the potential sites for my task.

After two days of searching, I concluded that I had found the ideal location, and the following afternoon I secured myself in a small clump of woods on a hill, overlooking the King's usual path. I had a four-hour wait, but eventually I saw the King upon his horse, bounding along the grass. It was obvious that the man had no real understanding of his steed. You could tell from his fastidious dress that he had never mucked out a stable in his life.

I raised my air-gun with the special extension and ammunition, and when the King was in position, I fired. My aim, as usual, was true. My pellet struck the King's horse directly on the rear, where it shattered upon impact. The horse started bucking, and after a few clumsy attempts to regain control, the King was thrown from his saddle and sent hurling into a cluster of large, sharp rocks.

After making sure that no one else was around (not even the frightened horse, who was galloping away on his own), I made my way down to examine the King. I'd hoped that he'd died instantly from the fall, but when I found him his neck was clearly broken, but he was still breathing. I hesitated a moment, trying to determine the best course of action, knowing that you were most insistent on this looking like an accident. Making up my mind quickly, I withdrew my handkerchief from my pocket, covered the lower portion of the King's face, and pinched his nose shut and kept my palm over his mouth. After a short period of thrashing, the King lay still, and I made plans to return to England as soon as possible.

   Checkmate, as the chess players say. The King is dead.

–S.M.

Holmes Meets the New King of Bohemia

If we accept the hypothesis that the King of Bohemia died between "A Scandal in Bohemia," and "A Case of Identity," then it seems that there were *three* incidents where Holmes engaged in a matter involving Irene Adler and the kingdom of Bohemia. The first occurred sometime before the events of "A Scandal in Bohemia," quite possibly as long as five years earlier, when Adler and the King first commenced their relationship. The relationship must have lasted long enough for the King to write a fair number of letters to Adler, but not long enough for there to be a slip allowing the relationship to leak out into the corridors of gossip. For the sake of convenience, we will assume that the relationship ended a little under five years earlier. This is enough time for Holmes' excellent memory to fade enough that he would need to consult his files to refresh his recollection of Adler's identity. But why was Adler in his files in the first place? According to Holmes himself in "His Last Bow," he was responsible for breaking up Adler and the King. This, then, was the first case that Holmes took on behalf of Bohemia regarding Irene Adler.

Roughly five years later, the King of Bohemia consulted Holmes about retrieving the photograph and letters from Adler. From his comments, and the fact that he did not know which man at 221B was Holmes and which was Watson, it is clear that the King did not know Holmes before meeting him that evening, and that the King had no idea that Holmes was involved in severing his relationship with Adler several years earlier. "A Scandal in Bohemia" was therefore the second case Holmes took on behalf of Bohemia connected to Irene Adler.

Based on the deductions and suppositions listed earlier, the King died a few months after the events of "A Scandal in Bohemia." In "A Case of Identity," Holmes displays a gold snuffbox with an amethyst that he received as a token of thanks for his work with the Adler papers. Yet Holmes professed to consider this case a failure, and his pride would not allow him to accept such a valuable gift for a job poorly done. Given his disdain for the King, and his refusal to take the emerald snake ring proffered by the King, it therefore appears that there was a third case involving Adler and Bohemia, but this time, Holmes acted on behalf of a different monarch whom he respected, the result was an unqualified success, and Holmes took pleasure in showing off the expensive trinket he received as compensation for his intervention. This was the third case Holmes took on behalf of Bohemia that involved Irene Adler.

But what happened in the first and third cases, about which we know nothing but the most basic details? For the answers to that, we must move beyond solid deduction from known facts and statements, and move into the realm of murky speculation. The sketch that follows is by no means meant to be the definitive truth, but it provides a reasonable explanation for a lot of the discrepancies that have been outlined in the previous chapters. The following tale is theoretical, and many of the specifics may be inaccurate, but the general heart of the story ought to mirror the truth.

•••

An account of Sherlock Holmes' visit to Bohemia, July or August of 1887

"Mr. Sherlock Holmes!" the King's equerry announced as the detective entered the isolated room in the castle.

Holmes recognized the man standing off to one side. He was the longtime Prime Minister of Bohemia, whom he had met about five years earlier. The other man bore a strong resemblance to his recently deceased elder brother, though his face was softer and perhaps kinder than his sibling's.

After a few brief words of welcome, the equerry exited and the three remaining men sat down in a cluster of lavishly embroidered but not very comfortable chairs. "Mr. Holmes," the Prime Minister said, "Thank you for coming to our country on such short notice."

"Not at all," Holmes replied. "My brother Mycroft made it clear to me that this meeting was of utmost importance to both our nations."

"Your esteemed brother did not exaggerate, Mr. Holmes," the Prime Minister nodded. "I was impressed by your work almost half a decade ago, when you managed to convince the previous King to sever his ties to Irene Adler without his knowledge of your influence."

"It was a simple matter," Holmes demurred. "At the time, I could hardly understand why my brother was so insistent that I address the matter myself. It was my pleasure to be of service, but the matter was so trifling that I put it out of my mind immediately. I did warn you that I could not guarantee that the last King had not sent Miss Adler some incriminating letters, as indeed, proved to be the case."

"Yes, and as I told you then, I assumed that even if he had, they would be of no consequence. Of course, I never believed that his late Majesty would be so love-struck as to allow a picture of himself to be taken with an adventuress of an opera singer, but even if he had, that would have been of no great consequence."

"Of course. I knew from the beginning that the late King was lying to me about the importance of that photograph. The Royal Family of Scandinavia enjoys its reputation for being straitlaced, but especially in this day and age, monarchs are realists. All the royal houses of Europe marry in order to cement alliances between nations, and love is not a primary motive. The fact that a potential royal bridegroom has a past that has not been as chaste as ice is of no consequence, provided that he is still capable of fathering heirs. It was obvious that not only did the late King want those papers for reasons other than covering up his relationship with Miss Adler, but that he wanted to keep the incident a secret from you as well."

The new King started to open his mouth, but before he could make a sound, the Prime Minister raised a finger, and the new King silenced himself. "Just how much do you know about this highly sensitive matter that has been a state secret for the past six years?" the Prime Minister asked.

"I *know* absolutely nothing," Holmes replied. "I *suspect* that the secret in question centers around some sort of major financial matter, possibly involving the collection of some valuable natural resource, and some situation that might lead to international tensions."

The Prime Minister's eyebrow arched, but only for a moment. "You are correct, Mr. Holmes. A little over six years ago, a team of geologists made a major discovery close to our southern border. Beneath an isolated valley is a substantial cache of oil. When sold to other nations, there is enough to swell the Bohemian coffers to bursting, placing our nation on a comfortable financial footing for many years, perhaps decades. But there is a delicate issue. The region where the oil is located is a contested area. By treaty, the location is undoubtedly part of Bohemia. Unfortunately, there are political forces in our neighbor to our south who believe that the region in question is by right part of their country. For years, our neighbor's government has had no desire to wage war to seize an area that they believe is filled with nothing but rocks and trees. But if they were to learn that a massive fortune in oil were located in that region..."

Holmes nodded. "They'd send troops to conquer the area in a matter of hours."

"Precisely. We are not trying to steal anything here; we are simply trying to keep what is ours. Soon after we made this discovery, we sent engineers to develop the most unobtrusive possible pumps and refineries to extract and ship the oil quietly and quickly. So far, this has been a rousing success. We have recruited an overseas company to help us sell the oil without outsiders knowing its source, and we have earned a magnificent profit. We knew that the oil supply would not last forever – our scientists tell us that at the current rate of extraction, we have less than two years before the oil runs out. We must keep the oil a secret until that time, and after that point it will not matter. Our southern neighbors will not wage war over a once-again worthless region."

"What role did the late King of Bohemia play in this matter, Prime Minister?"

"Very little. He had no head for business affairs, though he did recommend the foreign company that has managed the secret sale of the oil. I was surprised that he knew of such a business entity, but he managed to identify the perfect business for our purposes. I handled nearly all of the important details. Unfortunately, our constitution required me to keep him fully informed of the project, and five years ago one of my informants learned from reading the late King's ink-blotter that he had been revealing details to his then-paramour, Miss Adler. I advised him to watch his words, and he took umbrage at my warning. The late King had a quick temper, and when he overindulged in wine and spirits, he could be both loose-tongued and violent. Not only did I fear for the security of our state secrets, but I genuinely worried for Miss Adler's safety. It seemed to me that the best way to solve both problems was to terminate their relationship without the late King being aware of my influence. That is why I recruited you five years ago, and I was deeply grateful for your performance."

"It was nothing, Prime Minister. You mentioned that the late King suggested the foreign company that manages your oil interests. What was the name of this business, your Majesty?"

"The James Brothers, I believe. An English firm."

"The James Brothers!" Holmes' eyebrows shot upwards.

"You are familiar with them?" the new King asked.

"I am indeed. It has an excellent reputation, but as is often the case, appearances can be misleading. As is often the case, a shiny, flawless-looking apple may, once it is sliced open, prove to be rotten to the core. To most of the world, The James Brothers is one of the most respectable companies on the planet. But in reality, it is a front for a criminal organization run by the most fiendish mind on Earth– the Napoleon of crime, Professor James Moriarty!"

The Prime Minister blanched. "Are you certain of this, Mr. Holmes?"

"I am. I have spent over a year tracing Moriarty's influence to dozens of the most innocuous-looking companies, law firms, and small businesses in England. Taking its name from the fact that both the Professor and one of his siblings share the same Christian name– a point that must have caused no end of confusion in the Moriarty household when they were growing up – the James Brothers is a whited sepulcher. Beneath its reputable exterior, it is corrupt to the core. I have no doubt that they have been skimming greedily off the profits from the sale of the oil. Millions that ought to have gone into the Bohemian coffers are now funding the Moriarty gang. I have suspected for a long time that the Professor has been attempting to place members of European royal families and influential politicians under his control. I believe that the late King was one of the Professor's agents, though I cannot say if the deceased monarch was willingly recruited, or if he was somehow bullied or blackmailed into submission."

The Prime Minister pulled a handkerchief from his pocket and dabbed at his glistening forehead. "I wish that I could express incredulity at your accusation, Mr. Holmes, but you are confirming my suspicion that our former King was involved in some shady business that did not have the best interests of our nation at heart."

"I regret any distress that I inflict upon you, Prime Minister, but you should know that I also believe that Professor Moriarty was behind the late King's alleged 'accident' a couple of months ago."

The new King shuddered. "Am I in danger, Mr. Holmes?"

"I shall do my best to help protect you, Your Majesty. If I may shift the topic slightly, is the oil situation the true reason why the late King wanted me to retrieve the papers from Miss Irene Adler?"

"I believe so," the Prime Minister replied. "As I said, the late King leaked critical details about the oil extraction plan in his letters to Miss Adler, citing names of geologists and engineers he'd met with recently. These names meant nothing to her; they were simply men he'd met with recently as part of his royal duties, but to someone with specialist knowledge, it would completely give away the game. As for the photograph… never having seen it, I have no idea why he was so desperate to retrieve it."

"Prime Minister, there is something else in that photograph – the image of Professor Moriarty. He was inadvertently captured in the picture on a visit to discuss business with the King, and he is determined to retrieve it to eliminate any link between himself and Bohemian affairs."

The Prime Minister sighed. "I think you're right, Mr. Holmes. One of my spies recently informed me that there is an unknown but powerful figure who is determined to retrieve the papers from Miss Adler. If the information is correct, the woman –"

"*The* woman," Holmes thought to himself silently.

"– is in danger, and whatever secrets and information are hidden in those documents in danger of being captured by that figure, who is possibly, as you suspect, this Professor Moriarty. Mr. Holmes, will you please come to our nation's aid for a third time and make another attempt to retrieve the papers from Miss Adler – now Mrs. Norton?"

Holmes' lips formed a thin smile. "It would be my pleasure, Prime Minister."

•••

As stated earlier, the details of this narrative, such as the oil, are purely the best guesses of my imagination, but I strongly believe that the basic structure of the storyline approximates Holmes' work for the Bohemian government. Regarding the outcome of his third case on behalf of Bohemia involving Irene Adler, and how Holmes came to learn that Moriarty was in the photograph, my theories for what happened can be found in the next chapter.

A Theoretical Epilogue to 'A Scandal in Bohemia'

If we follow the clues sprinkled throughout the Canon, we can theorize that Holmes and Adler's paths did cross at least one more time, in order to protect her from the fallout of the case and to represent the interests of the government of the new King of Bohemia. So how did this meeting unfold? I shall once again move into the realm of speculation, though again I will stress that these ideas are extrapolated from evidence, rather than distilled from pure imagination.

Given Holmes' abilities, it's certainly conceivable that he might have tracked down Adler and her husband very soon after the government of Bohemia asked him to find her. But how could he earn her trust and convince her that he had been on her side all along? My best guess is that once he found her new address, he would leave a letter there while she was absent. When Adler returned, the message inside the envelope would read something a lot like this:

MY DEAR MISS IRENE ADLER:

I am not a man who is easily impressed, but I was greatly pleased by your actions at our last meeting. No doubt my words will surprise and confuse you. As you read these words, you are doubtless thinking to yourself that my supposed pleasure is a feint, a shameless attempt to preserve my vanity by contending that you did not outwit me at all, but instead behaved exactly as I had hoped you would. I can certainly understand your skepticism. After all, you are probably telling yourself, Sherlock Holmes would never fail if he could help it. You are asking yourself if this is a trick, some sort of psychological game I am playing upon you in order to regain my dominance and dignity. While this whole adventure of the "Scandal in Bohemia" has indeed been a massive charade, I assure you that not for one moment have I cast you as the villainess of the story.

I dare say that I have a great deal of work to do to earn your trust. That is understandable. Up until now, you have viewed me as an adversary, a mercenary-for-hire who is out to rob you of your leverage against a powerful man who has wronged you, an unfeeling agent of the Bohemian Crown with no regard for the indignity and emotional pain that the late King has inflicted upon you. You are certainly justified in harboring such suspicions. Indeed, it's quite logical for you to think the way you do. Logical, but wrong. Utterly and completely incorrect.

In order to commence the long journey towards winning your confidence, I shall have to start at the beginning. I think that you are laboring under the misconception that I only recently became aware of your existence. On the contrary, I have known of you, and your relationship with the late King, for some years now, ever since the Prime Minister of Bohemia hired me to arrange for the dissolution of your romantic relationship.

I can imagine the shock and indignation that you may be feeling at this moment. Surely this cannot be true! It is most assuredly the truth, but I hope that it will lessen the resentment you may feel towards me when I inform you that when I set in motion the chain of events that led to the severance of your liaison with the late King, I did so with the best of intentions. I was concerned not only with the geopolitical structure of Europe, but also with your safety. For if you had remained with the late King for much longer, you would have been drawn into a situation that even your cleverness and resourcefulness might have proven fruitless in escaping.

I think that you will believe me when I tell you that the late King was not a man who possessed the moral rectitude for leadership. No doubt the King's weak character was obvious to you by the end of your relationship. I wonder, though, did you ever suspect that the King was inextricably linked to a band of some of the most dangerous criminals in Europe?

I cannot provide too many details about how the King found himself in the clutches of a criminal gang, as that information includes official state secrets affecting multiple countries. I do suspect that you observed on multiple occasions that the King was acting in a distracted or temperamental manner. Perhaps you simply dismissed this behavior as part of the natural caprices of a man used to significant power, or the mood swings of a man whose crown has come to weigh too heavily upon his troubled head. I can tell you that over the past several years, the King has gradually become the leader of Bohemia in name only, as the criminal mastermind I cannot name has been manipulating the King to plunder the nation's treasury and resources, and the Bohemian Prime Minister has been compelled to go to superhuman lengths to keep the country together and solvent.

Not long before our meeting, the Prime Minister called upon me to continue my long-standing services for the Bohemian government to find out the cause of the hold that the criminal gang held over the King. I soon determined that the head of the criminal gang was obsessed with gaining control of the infamous photograph in your possession. At first I was confused by this, as the criminal mastermind already wielded sufficient power over the King to make the monarch his puppet. Further investigation led me to the revelation that the criminal organization's leader was afraid that he himself could be exposed by the photograph.

Have you ever really scrutinized the picture in your possession? Doubtless you feel little need to look at it often, as you have no desire to gaze at the image of the man who treated you so badly any more than necessary. If you had ever looked at the photograph through a magnifying lens, looking through the window on the left side of the image, you would see a reptilian-looking man. That is the criminal mastermind who bent the King of Bohemia to his will, who was captured visiting a place where he did not wish to be seen. This man knows that his relative anonymity is his greatest weapon, and a photograph that could potentially link him to the King would be detrimental to all of his plans.

(Please take a moment to go ahead and look at your copy of the picture. You need not worry about my watching you and determining its hiding-place, as I will soon demonstrate.)

That was the real reason the King was so desperate to retrieve the photograph. Not because he feared for his union to that Scandinavian princess! All royal families are pragmatists these days, and a relationship with an American opera singer would not doom a marriage that could benefit both nations. The King and his agents may have done their best to convince you that an appearance of propriety was at the heart of his desire to retrieve the photograph, but in actuality the King feared the anger of the man I not-so-fondly refer to as the Napoleon of Crime.

Blaming the King for allowing the photograph to be taken, the man I shall refer to as Napoleon for brevity's sake tasked the King with retrieving it. The King has appallingly inept henchmen. As you know, all of their previous attempts failed. So the King turned to me. He had no way of knowing that I had suspicions about his real reasons for wanting the photograph back.

You know much of the rest of the story, but I do not believe that you are aware of two other points. First, it was I who alerted you through a mutual acquaintance that I would likely be hired by the King. I wanted you to be alert to my presence on the case. Second, that I was your witness at your wedding. Yes! I imagine that comes as a shock to you. Unfortunately, as you will find out soon, it is not the gravest surprise I will be telling you about your marriage before this letter is finished.

But first, I need to put my actions on the day we met into full context. You know that it was I who staged the skirmish outside your home and made my way into your house in the guise of a clergyman. What you don't know is that your coachman was not so alert a guard as you had hoped. One of my colleagues ran to the window and distracted him for about fifteen seconds. It was enough time for me to leap up, sneak across the room, open the hiding-place, and use a small camera hidden in my coat to photograph the photograph! Before I replaced the picture, I took a quick look at it, and immediately noticed the face of Napoleon glowering through one the windows. I should point out that I was not certain of the real reason for the King's desperation to retrieve the photograph at this time, but as soon as I saw the picture, I knew why it was a danger to Napoleon's plans. Your coachman saw me standing on the side to of the room, so I hastily made my excuses and left.

At the risk of sounding as if I am desperate to trumpet my own cleverness, I must tell you that I was aware at once that you were following me! I was upwind of you, and I had smelled your distinctive perfume at the Church of St. Monica's and at your home, so I knew you were a short distance behind me. I reasoned that with Napoleon's men after the photograph and quite possibly you as well, it was safest for you to flee England. Since I was unlikely to convince you to do so by speaking to you directly,

I loudly told my dear friend Watson all that had transpired, making sure you overheard. When you wished me "good night" at my doorstep, my heart rejoiced, as I knew you would take the necessary steps to protect yourself.

I am not certain how much your housekeeper told you about my early morning visit to your home with Watson and the King, so forgive me if I repeat information that you are already aware of, please. Did you know that your home had been ransacked during the night, shortly after you left? This was the work of Napoleon's gang, who missed your leaving (you were wise to adopt another disguise) but searched your home in the hopes of finding the photograph or any evidence of where you might be heading. Once again, they lacked the ingenuity to find the hidden sliding-panel.

When I arrived at your home, I feigned shock at your absence, while secretly delighting in reading your letter, which confirmed all I had already deduced. I finished reading the letter long before the others, and I watched the King's changing face. His relief was obvious, but at first I was uncertain as to why. It was not until one of my associates signaled a message to me through the window using a form of sign language that my worst suspicions were confirmed. I insisted on having the King join me at your home so a couple of skilled operators of mine could search his rooms. There, they found the remains of a letter that the King believed he had burned. He had considered confessing all to the Prime Minister of Bohemia, but his nerve must have failed him and he destroyed the note. Enough of the document was salvageable to prove that not only was the King working with Napoleon, but that Napoleon had tasked the King with murdering the witnesses, including myself and yourself. Your absence and the removal of the photograph altered the situation, but I had been suspicious of the King ever since I noticed the firearm he was carrying in a holster, and the tiny fangs in his snake ring that indicated that it was designed to inject deadly poison into the unwary.

Incidentally, you may not be aware that when the King came to me, he accused you of extorting him with the photograph, ordering him to terminate his engagement or face exposure. I have no doubt that you are indignant at reading these words, and with good reason. Please rest assured that I determined very quickly that the King was lying, and you had no interest at all in meddling with his marriage. I know that your purpose in keeping the photograph was to protect yourself from repercussions, though unfortunately your possession of the photograph has led to consequences that you could not possibly have anticipated.

In any event, after brusquely leaving the King at your residence, I took steps to track you down. I had asked the King for your photograph, not out of sentiment, but to have a clear image of you to show to potential witnesses in an investigation to find you. You and Norton did a very capable job of hiding from the spotlight, but I was able to determine your location after a fairly short while, and use my agents to monitor you for the past few months.

No doubt you have heard of the King's recent passing. I can assure you that the reports of an accident are inaccurate. He was assassinated, and I wish to make sure that a similar fate does not befall you. Unfortunately, your connection to the late King puts you in mortal danger, and one of the two main sources of that peril comes from a source that is very close to you.

You will no doubt have noted that I addressed you at the beginning of this letter as "Miss Irene Adler." I believe it will cause you considerable distress to read what I am about to tell you, but unlike one young woman who came to me for help regarding a missing paramour recently, I believe that you are the sort of person who will not be destroyed by learning the truth about someone you love. The plain, blunt facts are these. You are not legally married to Mr. Godfrey Norton. The entire wedding was a pantomime to exploit you.

I am sure that a woman as perceptive as yourself has noticed the change in Mr. Norton over the last few months. The news of the King's death certainly came as a shock to him, as it upset the plans of his partners. You see, Mr. Norton and some of his business associates are aware of the delicate economic situation in Bohemia at this time, and they determined long ago to exploit it and get their cut of the profits. Your relationship with the King was not quite an open secret, but more people knew about it than you expected. A cabal of businessmen completely unrelated to Napoleon has been surreptitiously trying to gain a significant interest in the secret economic affairs of Bohemia, and they wished to gain control of your photograph in the hopes of blackmailing the King. After attempting various plans, and after Mr. Norton developed a rapport with you, he decided to pursue a romantic relationship with you... despite the fact that he already has a seriously ill wife in an asylum.

Due to the impending announcement of the King of Bohemia's engagement, Mr. Norton's bosses demanded that he secure his access to the photograph and you immediately, ideally through marriage. He was able to convince you to marry him in that sudden ceremony, and I believe that as an American with limited knowledge of English marriage laws regarding timing, witnesses, and the like, you were unaware that he was deliberately designing a fraudulent wedding that, if exposed, would protect him from a charge of bigamy. Any questions you might have had about a single witness or an informal license could be bluffed away by some plausible statement about changes to the law or the English doing things differently from Americans. The officiant at your wedding, as you may now suspect, was just as fraudulent a clergyman as I was. The real priest at St. Monica's was called away with a false story about a dying parishioner, and one of Norton's confederates donned the real priest's robes in order to perform a sham ceremony.

With the death of the King, Norton and his cronies no longer have the potential leverage they desire in order to profit from exploiting Bohemia's natural resources. As such, you are now much less valuable to them, and Napoleon still has you in his sights. You are in mortal danger, and I know that you have an additional concern. I wondered what Norton said to you to get you to marry him so abruptly, and after seeing you recently, I realized at once that there was a pressing reason for you to become a married woman as soon as possible. I know that a woman in your present condition may find flight difficult, and that you wish to avoid undue stress. Would you consider it an imposition if I were to offer my services, absolutely free of charge? I have no doubt that you are most capable of looking out for yourself, but if you choose to accept me as your ally, simply wave a handkerchief out of your north window and I shall be there at once to assist you in your escape. My connections to the British government will not only get you to a place of safety, but also will lead to the arrest of those who wish you ill. If you choose to trust me, and allow me access to the incriminating correspondence sent to you by the late King, I may be able to secure the economic future of the people of Bohemia as well.

I will freely confess to you that the Prime Minister and the new King of Bohemia have hired me to retrieve your letters from the late King, as a few of them contain oblique references to top-secret affairs of state. I will put no pressure on you. You can do what you wish with them.

If you are wondering how I can assure your safety, I will explain that for years I have perfected plans to fake one's own death. I dare say that I shall need to utilize such a plan myself one day, and if you are willing to allow the world to believe that you are deceased for a few years, I can help you escape the danger that pursues you.

You have thought of me as your enemy for many months, but I can assure you that I have always acted as your friend. However you wish to proceed, I remain, dear Miss Irene Adler,

Very truly yours,

SHERLOCK HOLMES

•••

Once again, I stress that this version of events is purely speculative, but it answers questions that the "A Scandal in Bohemia" leaves dangling, especially the problems inherent in the "wedding" of Adler and Norton. What happened to Adler after this point? Did she and Holmes meet again after this? There's no definitive evidence in the Canon, though countless fans and theorists have their ideas...

What Does Watson Know?

After considering all of the implications of what really happened in the case of "A Scandal in Bohemia," it's logical to wonder what the narrator of the story really knew. Did Watson know about Holmes' deliberate failure to retrieve the photograph, or did Watson genuinely believe that Holmes had truly been bested by Adler?

Ardent fans are fully aware that the real Watson is far more astute than the bumbling fool he is sometimes degraded as in adaptations and the popular imagination. He may not possess Holmes' detecting skills, but he is an intelligent man, and probably knows and understands Holmes better than anybody else on earth, with the possible exception of Mycroft. Could Watson have sensed that something was amiss, and played along?

It's certainly possible. Yet this theory is tempered by the fact that Watson is a fundamentally honest man, and his readers can rest assured that he strives to be as reliable a narrator as possible. It is not false modesty that compels Watson to record the many instances where he made false deductions or was fooled by one of Holmes' disguises, it is a commitment to accuracy that compels Watson to record details that paint him in an unflattering light.

In "The Empty House," Watson's fainting after Holmes revealed himself proved that Watson genuinely believed that Holmes had perished. Holmes often kept his closest friend out of the loop for his friend's own safety, and if Holmes led Watson to write a greatly exaggerated report of his own death for his own personal and professional purposes, then Holmes could similarly have fooled Watson into believing he had been beaten. As the events of "A Scandal in Bohemia" show, Holmes was a brilliant actor. His poor temper upon reading Adler's final missive was all a show put on for the benefit of an audience of two (possibly three if the housekeeper was still in the room), and Watson was too blindsided by this supposed turn of events to suspect that there was something deeper beneath the surface of the situation.

When Watson, after observing years of Holmes' dazzling triumphs, wrote in "A Scandal in Bohemia" that "So accustomed was I to his invariable success that the very possibility of his failing had ceased to enter into my head," there is a ring of truth to this. Perhaps this was another reason why Holmes decided to pull the wool over his associate's eyes. After all, an aura of infallibility may be impressive, but friendship is based on an equal footing, and it may have suited Holmes if his closest companion were to view him more as a human than as an unerring machine. As stated earlier, Holmes wanted to put the word out that he was capable of mistakes so as to lead his arch-nemesis into underestimating him, and it would have been better in Holmes' mind if Watson's report were written with the good doctor firmly believing it was the truth.

In the decades that followed, did Holmes and Adler's paths ever cross again? And whether they did or not, did Holmes ever reveal to Watson the real truth of "A Scandal in Bohemia," and beg Watson to remain silent? We'll never know for certain– there is simply no evidence to draw a solid conclusion from the Canon. All we have is speculation, and the hopes that eventually Holmes could entrust the whole truth of his secret cases to his dearest friend.

Conclusion – The Truth Behind 'A Scandal in Bohemia'

Sherlock Holmes' supposed most famous failure was actually a rousing success. Holmes' public humiliation was part of a very long game to bring down a powerful nemesis. Long before he faked his own death in order to assure the destruction of a dangerous criminal empire, he gave his own reputation a black eye in order to strengthen his position and assure his own long-term goals for justice. The supposed errors he made were too easily avoidable to be chalked up to clumsy mistakes. Allowing Irene Adler to get away with the incriminating photograph was not due to ineptitude, but by design.

Holmes had an ulterior motive when he took on the King's assignment, one which explained his seeming blunders and unusual behavior. This monograph makes no claims that the details of the theories propounded here are exactly what happened, but the spirit of the conjectures mirrors the actual truth of "A Scandal in Bohemia" far more accurately than the traditional interpretation of the narrative.

It should be noted that these new revelations about the case in no way impugn the character of Irene Adler. Her behavior was actually more moral and righteous as is generally assumed, since she was never a vengeful ex– looking for petty, exploitative payback towards a man who dumped her because she didn't have a royal pedigree. Her actions were clever, shrewd, and she acted with verve and daring. She was no villainess, and she proved herself to be a formidable woman. My reassessment of her character proves that she was a far less ethically dubious character than has long been supposed. The one feather in her cap that my analysis denies her stems from the fact that Adler never actually defeated Sherlock Holmes. "A Scandal in Bohemia" ended in exactly the way that Holmes wanted, although he could never actually admit that publicly.

If this monograph meets with a sufficiently high level of interest, I might explore Holmes' decision-making in "The Five Orange Pips," where his casual decision to send his client out into the night led to that young man's death. This could have been a simple error, but could this have all been part of a brilliant and devious long plan on Holmes' part, to save his client by faking his death and keeping the truth hidden from the world? It's possible. As over a century of Sherlockian pseudoscholarship has proven, there are countless hidden truths in the Canon that may be unveiled with a lot of close reading and creativity.

And so, the connection between Sherlock Holmes and "The Woman," Irene Adler, was something totally different from what has long been imagined by critics and fans. It was not a romance, as it has often been mischaracterized and distorted in many pastiches, nor was Holmes forever bound to her by the grudging respect paid to a triumphant rival. Holmes' professional interactions with Adler lasted longer than most readers ever suspected, as he interfered with her life years before "A Scandal in Bohemia" to sever her relationship with the King, and reconnected with her several months after her escape from England in order to tie up some loose ends for the benefit of the government of Bohemia and to extricate Adler from a dangerously complex situation. Ultimately, by "His Last Bow," Holmes was able to speak of his early involvement in Adler's life with pride, as a job well done that illustrated his long work with delicate international situations. In light of this new analysis of the events of "A Scandal in Bohemia," we must no longer view the tale as one of Holmes' failures, but instead as a great success, and part of a longer game to root out crime and corruption that ultimately led the supreme triumph of the great detective's career.

Also from MX Publishing

MX Publishing is the world's largest specialist Sherlock Holmes publisher, with over a hundred titles and fifty authors creating the latest in Sherlock Holmes fiction and non-fiction.

From traditional short stories and novels to travel guides and quiz books, MX Publishing cater for all Holmes fans.

The collection includes leading titles such as *Benedict Cumberbatch In Transition* and *The Norwood Author* which won the 2011 Howlett Award (Sherlock Holmes Book of the Year).

MX Publishing also has one of the largest communities of Holmes fans on Facebook with regular contributions from dozens of authors.

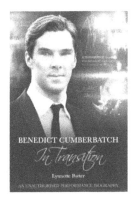

www.mxpublishing.com

Also from MX Publishing

The American Literati Series

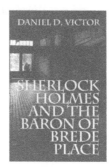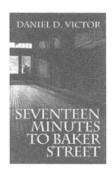

The Final Page of Baker Street
The Baron of Brede Place
Seventeen Minutes To Baker Street

"The really amazing thing about this book is the author's ability to call up the 'essence' of both the Baker Street 'digs' of Holmes and Watson as well as that of the 'mean streets' of Marlowe's Los Angeles. Although none of the action takes place in either place, Holmes and Watson share a sense of camaraderie and self-confidence in facing threats and problems that also pervades many of the later tales in the Canon. Following their conversations and banter is a return to Edwardian England and its certainties and hope for the future. This is definitely the world before The Great War."
Philip K Jones

www.mxpublishing.com

Also from MX Publishing

The Detective and The Woman Series

The Detective and The Woman
The Detective, The Woman and The Winking Tree
The Detective, The Woman and The Silent Hive

"The book is entertaining, puzzling and a lot of fun. I believe the author has hit on the only type of long-term relationship possible for Sherlock Holmes and Irene Adler. The details of the narrative only add force to the romantic defects we expect in both of them and their growth and development are truly marvelous to watch. This is not a love story. Instead, it is a coming-of-age tale starring two of our favorite characters."
Philip K Jones

www.mxpublishing.com

Also from MX Publishing

The Sherlock Holmes and Enoch Hale Series

The Amateur Executioner
The Poisoned Penman
The Egyptian Curse

"The Amateur Executioner: Enoch Hale Meets Sherlock Holmes", the first collaboration between Dan Andriacco and Kieran McMullen, concerns the possibility of a Fenian attack in London. Hale, a native Bostonian, is a reporter for London's Central News Syndicate - where, in 1920, Horace Harker is still a familiar figure, though far from revered. "The Amateur Executioner" takes us into an ambiguous and murky world where right and wrong aren't always distinguishable. I look forward to reading more about Enoch Hale."
Sherlock Holmes Society of London

Also from MX Publishing

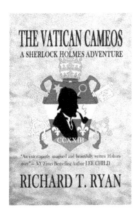

When the papal apartments are burgled in 1901, Sherlock Holmes is summoned to Rome by Pope Leo XII. After learning from the pontiff that several priceless cameos that could prove compromising to the church, and perhaps determine the future of the newly unified Italy, have been stolen, Holmes is asked to recover them. In a parallel story, Michelangelo, the toast of Rome in 1501 after the unveiling of his Pieta, is commissioned by Pope Alexander VI, the last of the Borgia pontiffs, with creating the cameos that will bedevil Holmes and the papacy four centuries later. For fans of Conan Doyle's immortal detective, the game is always afoot. However, the great detective has never encountered an adversary quite like the one with whom he crosses swords in "The Vatican Cameos.."

"An extravagantly imagined and beautifully written Holmes story"
(Lee Child, NY Times Bestselling author, Jack Reacher series)

CPSIA information can be obtained
at www.ICGtesting.com
Printed in the USA
BVHW071722080121
597272BV00007B/409